Slocum, drink in hand, watched Jamie start for the door. The Kid wasn't going to waste any time in his effort to mow down Hook Fulton. Yet something looked comic in the way Jamie's young slender body moved, hunched and determined. That was how it seemed to strike the red-faced cowboy, sitting at a nearby table with a glass in his hand. He smirked and, in mischief, stuck out his booted leg, tripping Jamie, which sent him toward the floor. But as the Kid hit it, he turned. His gun was suddenly in hand and there was a crack of gunfire and the splintering of glass as the drink spattered. The red-faced cowboy's eyes were wide in shock as he stared at the tenderfoot on the floor, still holding his gun...

OTHER BOOKS BY JAKE LOGAN

JAKE LOGAN

SLOCUM AND THE AVENGING GUN

BERKLEY BOOKS, NEW YORK

SLOCUM AND THE AVENGING GUN

A Berkley Book/published by arrangement with
the author

PRINTING HISTORY
Berkley edition/July 1985

ISBN: 0-425-07973-2

A BERKLEY BOOK ® TM 757,375
Berkley Books are published by The Berkley Publishing Group,
200 Madison Avenue, New York, N.Y. 10016.
The name "BERKLEY" and the stylized "B" with design are trademarks
belonging to Berkley Publishing Corporation.

PRINTED IN THE UNITED STATES OF AMERICA

1

Slocum smiled at Lulabelle lying naked on the bed, a picture of grace and sex. But again he caught that hard glitter in her blue eyes, something he didn't particularly care for. They'd been wrestling amorously on that bed for the longest time, during which she had squealed, screeched, and moaned as he played manfully on her white, firm, beautifully shaped body. But now that it was over, she had that curious look in her eyes again. He just couldn't figure her out.

They had met two hours before at Riley's Saloon and Dance Hall, where she'd been belting Dixie songs for the cowboys, which touched his Georgia heart. He introduced himself, John Slocum of Calhoun County, and told her he enjoyed the songs. She gazed at him with those glowing blue eyes while he gazed at the plump swelling of her white bosom. Then she seemed to cotton to him: it could be his accent, or whatever, but after a few drinks, she told him nothing would give her more pleasure than to spend private time with him at her hotel, and he took it as a fine personal compliment.

She disappeared for five minutes, then took his arm and led him to her room at the O.K. Hotel at the end of town, where she peeled and showed a beautiful body. In the room, he had kissed her plump breasts, stroked the curves of her shapely body, and she came on fire like a torch.

She went for his lusty flesh with a fierce appetite, they made riotous love, and now he was getting dressed while she stayed nude. She watched him, he thought, not quite like a satisfied woman, more like a cougar eyeing its prey. Too much to figure out, so he just said, "Lulabelle, it's been a honey time meeting you, and it's a pity I have to leave."

Her eyes narrowed. "Like to say the same, Slocum, but there's no need to run. Lovers like you are scarce as hens' teeth."

"Women like you are, too." His eyes went over her curvy white body.

Just then the door opened and a slender cowboy came in. He stopped short, his eyes goggling at the sight of the naked Lulabelle. His gaze swung to Slocum, and his face went into a fearful scowl. He had light skin, a blondish moustache, and gray eyes that blazed with jealousy.

Slocum tensed; he looked like a tenderfoot whose feelings could quickly stampede his brains.

"What the goddamn hell is goin' on here, Lulabelle? What's this cowboy doin' here? Why'd you send for me?"

Slocum stiffened. Why in hell *did* she send for him?

Cool as a cucumber, Lulabelle said, "Whatever do you think is goin' on, Jed?"

Jed gulped twice and scowled fiercely. "I tole you, Lulabelle, I want you for my woman. And I don't aim to let any tumbleweed cowboy stomp in here and mess things up." His white face had gone red with rage as a glance at the bed revealed that a hell of a lot of red-hot action had gone on before his entrance.

Slocum stared at Lulabelle; the treacherous little bitch had sent for Jed, and she had to have some miserable reason.

Jed's gray eyes were clouded with fury. "Who the hell are you, cowboy, and what are you doin' in this room?"

Slocum's instincts were alert. The dude looked ferocious, like a frustrated rooster ready to peck his rival to pieces. The lady Lulabelle was something of a trickster and had brought them together for plenty of mischief. It would be a good idea to soothe the dude's ruffled feathers, or something unfortunate could happen.

"Well, sonny, the name is Slocum. And I suggest you don't get all riled up. The lady's free to do as she pleases. Seems like you got no claim here."

Jed's eyes glinted like ice. "I figure you're jumpin' my claim, Mr. Nobody-from-nowhere. You're trying to put a brand on my woman." He stepped deliberately in front of the door. "I say you made a bad mistake."

There was a long moment of silence, then Slocum said, "Step aside, little cowboy. I aim to go out that door now."

"There's only one way you're goin' out that door, you lowdown, rustling hyena. Flat out."

Slocum looked into the cold, threatening face, then glanced at Lulabelle. She was watching fascinated, her eyes glazed with the expectation that within moments Slocum would be shot.

"Don't be dumb, Jed," he said. "You're playing her game. She wants a shootin'."

"That's what she's goin' to get," he snarled, " 'cause

you ain't goin' outa this room breathin'." Jed's hands dropped down to his side.

"Are you loco?" Slocum said. But it was already too late. Slocum watched Jed's gray, rage-filled eyes suddenly narrow as his hands darted down to his gun. The sound of a pistol shot filled the room.

Jed was flung against the door, a neat bullethole in the center of his forehead. He fell, sitting down, the expression of rage petrified on his face in death.

Slocum put his gun back in its holster. "The damned idiot pulled his gun. What could I do?" he said, mostly to himself. He never dreamed his game with Lulabelle would end like this.

He pulled the body away from the door, ready to get the hell out.

"Stop right there, Slocum," Lulabelle said.

She had a deadly smile and a derringer in her hand. Must have had it under the mattress.

"Throw your gun," she ordered. He dropped it and stared at her; still naked, she had moved near the chair where her chemise lay.

"You sent for Jed, didn't you?" he said.

Her smile was vicious. "Yeah, I sent for him. I thought he'd shoot your brains out. That was a mistake." She glanced at the body, but there was little feeling in her hard, pretty face.

Slocum scratched his head. "What the hell have you got against me, Lulabelle? I've done you no mischief."

Her eyes glowed like ice. "Oh, you did me a lotta mischief. In Bragg City, two months ago, John Slocum shot Dan Young. I swore on my knees to get revenge. And you're John Slocum."

He sat limply on the bed. It was true, he had shot

Dan Young, but that damned outlaw had just robbed the bank in Bragg City and, trying to escape, killed a man and a woman in the street. Slocum shot him off his horse as he was racing out of town.

"Who's Dan Young to you?" he demanded.

"He was my man," she said fervently.

"Dan Young deserved to die," he said. "He killed Amos Steele and Liza Calder during a robbery."

There was a long pause. "Well," she said, "you ain't goin' off scot free. You see, you just killed Jed Davis, the beloved son of Judge Hiram Davis."

His eyes widened. "Hanging Judge Davis?"

"The same. So you can count on a necktie party within the hour, *Mister* Slocum."

He shook his head in disbelief, and with one fast movement flung the pillow at her derringer and plunged after it. He wrested the small gun from her hand while she fought fiercely and cussed.

"You shouldn't play with dangerous toys, Lulabelle," he said. He pinned her arms behind her, tied them with one of several thin leather thongs he carried in his hip pocket, then put a kerchief in her mouth.

He picked up his gun, walked to the door, and smiled. "Stick to lovin', Lulabelle. You're better at it than revenge. As for Dan Young, he was a no-good killer outlaw, and you're better off without him."

He opened the door. A thin, bespectacled clerk stood outside.

"What's the shootin', sir?" he asked.

"Gun went off. Nothing serious. Lulabelle wants you to wake her in a couple hours." He smiled, shut the door, and went down to the roan, mounted up, and trotted out of town.

• • •

They came after him, a posse of four men, but they didn't seem to have their hearts in the riding. For one thing, he had led them to the edge of the desert, and under the broiling sun they couldn't be all-fired happy about pursuit. And maybe Jed Davis didn't seem to them worth all the trouble.

Hours later, after he moved them onto the dry dust, he saw them hot and drooping, holding a powwow, practically squeezing their canteens. One of their horses had gone lame, too.

They glared at him, far away and on a rise, then shot their guns into the air, as if to say he could rot in the New Mexico Territory if he wanted; they were heading back.

He smiled. Most of that night he traveled in the cool until he reached the Santa Fe trail. He was almost dried out before he found a water hole, collected the water carefully in his hat, and let the roan drink first.

He rode southwest for two days. The land turned green and grassy. When he found a small sparkling stream, he wet down the roan and put him out to graze in a rich patch of grass. Then Slocum frolicked in the water in his skin, cleaning off sweat and caked dirt. Afterward, he fried a jackrabbit that had the misfortune to catch his eye, and made coffee. Refreshed in body and spirit, he again rode southwest into the grassy land.

He was high on a rise when he saw Hook Fulton and his bunch going north. They rode single file, and Slocum took a quick breath, thinking he might have stumbled on Apaches. But it was Hook, easy to recognize in his forked black hat and on his piebald. The men behind him were big, bulky, tough looking. Slocum had seen them in Abilene. What ornery mischief, he wondered, were they up to? Horse-rustling or bank-robbing? The tense way they rode left him curious, so, for a time, he followed, keeping out of sight. When they rode past a corral where the horses would have made good rustling, it surprised him. They had better game in mind, probably. But there was small profit in trailing Fulton, other than curiosity, when he himself was headed for Santa Fe.

It was a pitiless sun in a brassy sky, and the heat bounced off the rocks. Too hot, Slocum figured, to travel at a time like this. He found cover among the rocks and decided to doze during the blistering heat and travel later, when the sun started down.

He slipped into a doze and found himself caught up by a beautiful naked woman wearing a mask. Her body with its plump, cherry-tipped breasts and dark fuzz between the thighs looked familiar, and she held out her arms to him. His flesh grew fierce and lusty, and when he started for her, she grinned, pulled off the mask, and aimed her derringer straight at his erection. Her laugh sounded like the grating on rocks. His eyes shot open. Thirty feet away was a cougar, its bullet-shaped body crouched, as it put one paw in front of the other, its black eyes gleaming.

Slocum's hand crept to his gun and the cougar, with its powerful instinct for survival, halted, as if suddenly aware that the object he contemplated as a meal had become a fearful enemy. The black eyes that had glowed viciously now looked bewildered, and the cougar seemed to smell its own death in the pointed iron, for it wheeled abruptly and slunk quickly behind a cover of rocks. Slocum listened to the soft patter of its claws as it disappeared.

Slocum took a long breath, glad he didn't have to shoot. In such close encounters, if you didn't hit the brain you could be clawed to death.

He looked at the cougar's tracks and, satisfied it was safe, he pulled beef jerky and munched it. Then he saw the smoke in the east, and it alerted him to Apaches. He rode west, keeping the high ground. As he rode, his thoughts returned to the posse sent after him by Hanging Judge Davis. It would have been a disaster if they got their hands on him, mostly because the judge must have given instructions to lynch him on the spot. Lulabelle would never testify that Jed had provoked the fight or that Jed had drawn his gun.

It was just as well that he was moving toward the New Mexico Territory, an area lawmen didn't go into much.

On the other hand, it was Apache country, and he could still see the smoke on the horizon. Apaches talking smoke was never a good sign. He'd fought redskins of many tribes and, in his experience, found the Apache was the cleverest, meanest, most dangerous of them all. Raised to be a warrior, he was trained to be cunning, courageous and merciless. Traveling this lonely country kept Slocum steadily alert for Apache tracks.

The sun was now golden orange in a brilliant sky, and he looked at the soaring rocks, the scrub pine, the boulders spotting the plain beneath him. A hawk swooped from its perch, aimed like a bullet at its prey, lizard, maybe.

Then Slocum heard the gunshot.

The sound bounced off the rocks and was followed

by three other shots. Instinctively, he ducked, though he couldn't be the target. The gunfire came from below, on the trail, and from his concealed view he could see the opponents. Hook Fulton and his five men had flung themselves off their horses and were squatted behind boulders. And firing at them, also behind boulders, were a cowboy and a blonde woman whose hair caught the sun in a blaze of gold. Slocum scowled and, even as he reached for his rifle, not yet knowing what he would do, he frowned at the inequality of the gun battle. From the look of it, the cowboy and the girl had trailed Hook and his men and tried to ambush them.

They were not too far apart, about fifty yards, and the land was pockmarked with boulders, trees, and tall grass—good cover for a bushwhacking.

But two against five, and such men as these, made it most probable that it would end badly. It didn't take much for Slocum to picture what had happened. Hook Fulton was a predator, a hyena, and he'd probably done a great mischief to the cowboy and the woman. Otherwise, why would they make such a reckless attack? Still, Slocum couldn't help being surprised by the cowboy's sharp shooting. He wore a black Stetson and checked shirt, scuffed boots, and used a Colt. His every shot seemed to miss by inches, and made Hook's men sweat, swear, and jump.

As he expected, Hook eventually signaled one man to try an encirclement, but he made the mistake of exposing his body for just an instant. The cowboy picked him off in a flash and he lurched back as if he'd been kicked by a two-ton mule.

Hook Fulton gave careful instructions to another

man, big, beefy, black-shirted, who crawled on his belly back about fifty yards till he reached a cluster of rocks. He worked his way in a big circle, far behind the two, then kept crawling forward, always under cover.

Slocum had been too far to do any good, but he, too, worked his way down the ridge, carefully, keeping his rifle tight in hand.

Hook Fulton, aware his man was closing in, threw lots of lead to keep the cowboy concentrated and under cover. The ruse worked, because the beefy man, crouched low, came from behind a boulder, his gun pointing. His voice rang out harshly. "Throw your guns or I'll blow your heads off."

For a moment the cowboy looked as if he'd try to shoot it out, but a glance at the woman made him stop. They dropped their guns.

"Good work, Wild Bill!" yelled Hook, coming forward, followed by his men, big and bulky, all grinning. Slocum didn't like the look of it. He kept coming down, expecting the worst.

Still, it happened so fast he was caught by surprise. Wild Bill bent to the guns, threw them away, and with the same movement grabbed the blonde and threw her over his shoulder. The slender cowboy, in a rage, rushed him, but Wild Bill dropped the girl and flung the cowboy back hard against the rocks, which stunned him. He fell, still.

The blonde started to run and Wild Bill caught her, wrestled her to the ground where she struggled fiercely under him. In the struggle, her shirt tore, and her breasts came into view.

Wild Bill's laugh was evil as he held her pinned

to the ground and looked toward Hook Fulton.

Slocum, who, until this moment, had hoped Fulton would interfere, felt a rush of fury, brought his rifle sight to his eye, and hit the shoulder of the man to stop him.

He howled, grabbed his shoulder, and looked at the high rocks. The girl, in a fury, moved with amazing speed. She grabbed Wild Bill's gun from its holster and put a bullet in his chest; it bloomed with blood. She flung him off her body, turning, as if all she wanted was to kill Fulton. But he coldly shot her, and she fell back, stone dead. Then Fulton whipped around, shot up at the rocks at Slocum, shaking with rage, ready to fire, but he had to duck. They had him located, and were shooting all around, which kept him down. He crawled to another boulder, in a fury at himself because he'd lost Fulton. He caught a movement of one man peering from behind a rock, and his bullet exploded pieces of rock in the face. Again they threw a spew of bullets at him and he hunkered down.

When he peered out, he no longer had a target, for the men skulking behind the boulders had reached their horses. They were behind too much cover now as they rode for him to do much good, but he fired anyway to keep them riding. They were heading southwest.

He took a deep breath and started down to where the cowboy was cradling the girl in his lap, his face covered with tears.

The cowboy, when he saw Slocum, brushed at his tears, and his jaw hardened. He was young, still beardless, handsome, with intense blue eyes and yellow hair that peeped from his short-brimmed black hat. A smooth-handled Colt peered from its holster, and his black boots were scarred. Slocum felt instantly that there was plenty of guts and feeling in this cowboy.

"Your girl?" he asked gently.

"Sister." Again the blue eyes misted.

Slocum moved to his saddlebag, pulled out his shovel, and began to dig, to give the cowboy time to compose himself.

The cowboy didn't speak again until the girl had been buried, and after Slocum had mumbled over the grave, "The good die young, and those whose hearts are mean grow rotten with time." Slocum pulled a pint from his saddlebag and gave it to the cowboy.

The kid gulped some, coughed, wiped his mouth. "What's your name?" he asked, his face hard.

"Slocum. John Slocum."

"Mr. Slocum, I want to thank you. You really helped. If only you'd shot that slimy hyena before he killed Cathy." He took another short drink. "I'm Jamie O'Neill."

"That slimy hyena was Hook Fulton," Slocum said, taking a short pull from the bottle.

The kid's eyes glittered with hope. "Do you know him?"

"Yes, I know him. Wanted in Missouri and Texas for bank robbery, rustling, murder."

Jamie took his hat off and his short yellow hair, like his dead sister Cathy's, burned in the sun. "Hook Fulton," he said, his face twisting with hate. "If it's the last thing I do in life, I will kill that piece of slime. I take a holy oath."

Slocum felt a stab of feeling at Jamie's words. "To tell the truth, Jamie, I don't think you and Cathy acted with good judgment, just the two of you taking on Hook Fulton's bunch."

Jamie glared. "Wasn't a matter of judgment. They killed my father and kid brother."

Slocum looked into the blazing blue eyes and felt a wave of sadness. He turned to look at the sinking sun, which left the sky glowing red and orange. The mountain peaks thrust against the sky like cathedral steeples. Just now the world looked like a holy place, where evil would be impossible. But this young cowboy had just had his entire family wiped out: sister, father, brother. And by a cutthroat, a killer who deserved to be boiled in oil.

It had to be money. From what he knew about Fulton, he was spurred mostly be greed.

"What made Fulton pick on your people, Jamie?"

"It was robbery," Jamie said, and looked at Slocum. "I thank you again for your help. Now I'm goin' after Hook Fulton, and, before God, I swear to never stop till he or me is dead."

Slocum watched the young cowboy walk toward his horse, a sturdy, deep-chested black. His heart went out to the cowboy.

"Hold it," he said.

Jamie turned, his face in a frown. He looked so young, so vulnerable, even though he could shoot like a demon.

"Wouldn't you like some help, Jamie?"

The cowboy stared. His fierce blue eyes seemed to light up with inner fire.

"Hook Fulton," he said, "sounds like a poisonous rattler. And this ain't your quarrel, Slocum. But..." He stopped, and bit his lips.

"It's my quarrel," Slocum said with a small smile.

"My quarrel is with any poisonous rattler I happen to meet." He shifted his gunbelt. "I think you'll do better with my help."

The cowboy's lips twisted in a painful smile. "I think so, too."

2

They rode hard, following the trail left by the Fulton bunch, but they couldn't make much headway. The sun was low in the sky, forcing them to think of camp before dark.

"I suppose," said Slocum, "it wouldn't hurt to pick off something for eating."

The Kid—and Slocum had begun to think of Jamie as the Kid—looked at him, then turned. His gun came out with dazzling speed and barked. Fifty yards away a pheasant fell. Slocum smiled; the Kid was a demon with the gun. He'd hate to come up against him. He had the quickest reflexes and a sharpshooter's eye.

They camped near a rivulet, and Slocum dug a deep pit to hide the fire. "There's Apaches in the high east country," he said.

"I've seen the smoke," the Kid said. He sipped coffee and his eyes looked brooding. It had to be a rough time for him. He looked like a wounded animal, hurt beyond all cure, lying on his bedroll, his hands behind his head, staring up.

A quarter moon was climbing slowly in the sky, and Slocum watched it, and the stars, big as a man's fist break out against the dark blue. To lose one's whole family like that in twenty-four hours, Slocum

thought, had to be the worst thing that could happen
to a man. It didn't surprise him that during the night
the sound of crying reached him. Every once in a
while, he heard the sharp intake of breath, of a man
in pain, then the flow of curses.

Slocum gritted his teeth and thought about Hook
Fulton. Once, in Abilene, Slocum had played poker
with a hard-eyed, scarfaced big man who lost a wad
in a hurry. He didn't like it, and smoothly insinuated
that nobody could have that kind of luck. Slocum
turned icy and asked politely, "You suggesting, mister,
that I play crooked cards?"

There was a freezing moment while the scarfaced
man looked hard, and it seemed like he was ready to
say the wrong thing. Then one of the players said,
"Hey, Hook, why can't you lose like anyone else
without thinkin' it has to be tricks?"

The scarface glared at him, then grinned suddenly.
It had been the right note to ease the tension. "You're
right, Charlie. This cowboy plays good poker, and
I've got no beef. What's the handle, mister?"

"Slocum. John Slocum."

"Well, Slocum, if you shoot like you play cards,
it'd be nice to have a man like you in our bunch. If
you ever feel you'd like to join up, ask for me, Hook
Fulton. Folks know me."

Folks knew him all right. He had an evil rep even
then. They said he robbed banks with the James gang,
was wanted for killings in Kansas City, even that he'd
shot the Colorado Kid in the back.

And Hook Fulton was the man that the Kid, Jamie
O'Neill, had sworn to wipe out.

Slocum twisted in his bedroll. It wasn't going to
be easy.

• • •

They picked up Fulton's tracks next morning, and to close the distance, they rode hard. But Hook and his men had also been pushing their horses, and it didn't take much imagination to figure out why. Apache smoke signals had to be unnerving.

Slocum, as he rode, couldn't help but note the hard set of the Kid's jaw, his glazed eyes, as if, in his mind, he was working out the most vicious revenge on Hook Fulton.

For his part, Slocum focused on the trail, his piercing green eyes raking the ridges, boulders, shape of the land, looking always for the telltale hostile clue. He'd been blessed by nature with sharp sight and quick intuition. It was why he survived in a territory that bristled with danger and sudden death.

It was just such intuition that made him steer the roan sideways to the shelter of a declining cliff, as they approached a ridge that would give a bushwhacker, if one was there, shooting command of the trail. The Kid, preoccupied with his thoughts, continued riding straight. Suddenly a rifle roared and the black buckled under him and fell. Slocum's gun was out and firing at the rifleman behind the ridge edge. He ducked, giving Jamie time to jump clear of the fallen horse, roll over till he found shelter behind a half-sunk rock in the earth.

Slocum, his eyes fixed on the jagged edge of the ridge, brought the roan into shelter, then stood motionless, holding his breath, his finger on the trigger. It was hard for Slocum to keep steady because of the rage that shook his body. Only a rotten hyena of a man would shoot a horse, and he ached fiercely for a chance to blow the man's head off.

But, for whatever reason, the bushwhackers didn't show. Might be they feared the sharpshooter below might hit this time. Might be they felt the job was done, since two men on one horse could never catch up.

By this time, the sun had dipped behind the soaring mountain peaks, and shooting long distance could no longer be accurate.

Still, they were pinned down, and Slocum waited a bit longer for the light to fade, then began to crawl forward. Now he heard hoofbeats faint in the distance: two horses, going southwest.

The siege was over. He looked down at the horse breathing painfully, still alive; it had been gutted by a stupid, blundering gunman who intended to hit the rider. It suffered, and Slocum, jaw hard, waited for Jamie to put his animal out of its misery. But Jamie turned away, his face pale.

"Do it," he said, and stalked off.

Slocum bent, put a bullet in the animal's brain, and vowed vengeance.

It was noon of the next day with the sun like a red-hot eye in the scalded sky when Slocum caught the strange gleam on the plain near a steep rising slope of the mountain.

He gritted his teeth and studied the land surrounding it, two heavy high-flying birds, vultures. He shook his head. "Stand ready," he muttered to Jamie riding behind him.

"What is it?" asked Jamie with a frown.

"You'll see soon enough," grunted Slocum. The Kid was softer than he expected—his youth, probably—and there was no point in working on his nerves.

After twenty minutes of riding they found what he had suspected: two men, scalped, tied to the ground, eyes pinned open. A great swarm of red ants had crawled into the eyes and over every inch of the dead men. Though the ants had already done a horrendous job, the men were recognizable to Slocum: they were Gleason and Baker of the Fulton bunch.

It was not the nicest thing in the world to look at, and the Kid gagged and turned away. Jamie could shoot like a demon, but he had a delicate gut. Slocum's piercing green eyes examined the tracks, followed them until they went behind a big boulder that gave a clear view of the trail from east to west. The signs, to Slocum, were as clear as reading a book. He pieced it together like this: Hook Fulton, aware that Jamie O'Neill, burning with revenge, would trail him, backed up perhaps by the stranger who had shot Wild Bill from the slope, had put Gleason and Baker behind this boulder to do ambush. Hook's mistake was not to figure on the Apaches, who did a bit of their own ambushing. It didn't take long for the Apaches to amuse themselves: a few artistic flesh cuttings to enjoy the paleface cowardice, and, after the game became boring, they laid the desperadoes out, spread-eagled, naked, and laced with honey to lure the big red ants.

Slocum studied the land, his eyes restless, his senses alert. He knew the two men lying there, Gleason and Baker, had been lowdown, rotten skunks in their lifetime, but nobody deserved to die like this. But the Apache, a merciless warrior, dealt out violent death to the paleface who stole his land.

Slocum shook his head; the worst thing for a white man was to fall into the hands of an avenging Apache. Better by far to die by arrow or bullet before that.

Slocum looked hard at the moccasin tracks and judged that at least four Apaches had killed Gleason and Baker. The redskins had to be nearby, and his green eyes, sharp and penetrating, casually scanned the rocks high to his right. Indians loved the high ground.

There—a slight movement! His pulse quickened; they were being observed. His mind worked feverishly. If they rode along the trail as the Apaches rightly figured, they'd be sitting ducks for crossfire. But a sharp turn west offered a clearing and a crevice which would make excellent shelter, if they could get there. The Apaches expected them to pick up the trail and, if he swung toward that crevice, they'd be puzzled for only a few moments. Then, when they figured his intentions, they'd race out in a howling charge.

"We got company," he said in an undertone to the Kid, wheeling the roan to the clearing.

Jamie's eyes shocked open. "Redskins!" he muttered.

"They're watching us. We ride nice and easy, straight ahead, and when we get to the crevice, go hard for it. If they come, turn sharp and shoot. Make the shots count. We won't get them in the open for more than a few moments."

While he jogged the roan toward the clear, he felt his heart thump and his body expected the thud of a bullet, but there was only silence. Slocum wondered if he had read it all wrong. Then he saw them, all four, appear at the top of the rise.

They wore bands around their long hair, held rifles and bows, and suddenly the air split with their cries as they galloped down.

He raced the roan toward the crevice, but turned

to fire at an Apache, his rifle raised for sighting. The bullet hit his chest and jerked him off his horse. The Apache right behind reined his pony sharply to keep it from trampling the fallen warrior. The Kid shot him dead center in the chest, and he stiffened, then fell sideways. A bullet hit Slocum's saddlebag, fired by the Apache on a spotted mustang. He had raised his rifle again when Slocum's bullet hit him and he tottered on his horse like a doll whose sawdust had just run out. The one Apache left pulled roughly at his pony, forced it into a turn, fiercely thumped it, and raced into the shelter of the rocks.

Slocum watched him, thinking hard.

"Let's go," Jamie said. "We're through with them."

Slocum's face was grim. "What about the one who got away?"

"To hell with him. It's Hook Fulton we want."

Slocum rubbed his chin, thinking that a single Apache roaming free, especially one who'd seen his comrades fall, could be as dangerous as a dozen. But to go after him would be long, tough tracking, and Hook Fulton was the target.

"All right," he said.

The horses belonging to Gleason and Baker, and taken by the Apaches, were grazing nearby. He rode to the big black, caught its reins, and brought it back to Jamie. The young cowboy swung easily over the saddle, turned to Slocum, still hard-faced. He spoke grimly, and fire blazed in his blue eyes. "Now let's get Hook Fulton."

For the next few hours, as they tracked Hook Fulton, they kept the horses on a steady jog. The sun still pounded down blistering heat, though it was late afternoon. To their left the great mountain range towered, its jagged peaks thrusting up in a valiant effort to escape the earth. Slocum's body was drenched with sweat, and sweat gleamed on the haunches of the roan. When finally they reached a small stream, Slocum wet down the roan, then peeled his clothes and plunged in. The Kid, who didn't seem to sweat much, wet his black, kept watch, and used his bandanna to freshen himself.

They ate beef jerky and drank coffee.

The Kid seemed restless. "We should be moving." His voice was hard.

Slocum shook his head. "No use abusing the horses. When we want them to run, they won't be able to."

"Hook's not worried about *his* horses," the Kid said grimly.

"Hook's a hyena, not a man," Slocum said, leaning against a boulder. He took out a havana and lit it. "Can one ask, Jamie, where you happened to be when Hook and his men hit your place?"

The Kid looked surprised at the question, then, as the memory of it came back, his face darkened. "Me and Cathy were up in the hills, tending a cow that was calving. We heard the shots, raced to the house, but it was all over by then." His handsome face hardened, and the light blue eyes glittered. "We found Dad on the floor, shot in the face and chest. And Johnny dead, too. He was near the rifle on the mantle."

There was a long silence. "Why'd they hit your place?" Slocum wondered. "Seems queer."

"What d'ye mean, queer? I told you, it was robbery."

"Well, they rob banks, rustle horses, cattle, but it's all big stuff."

Jamie shrugged. "They robbed us."

Slocum blew smoke into the air. "Did your father have money?"

"He had money."

"Like what?"

"Twenty-five thousand dollars."

Slocum scowled. "You serious?"

"That's what he had."

"How in hell did he get that kind of money?"

Jamie shrugged. "Always had it, seems to me. Didn't care to spend it, but wanted us to have it, a nest egg."

Slocum flicked the havana, watched it somersault to the earth. "If he didn't spend, how did Hook know about it?"

Jamie's fist clenched. "That's the mystery. It's something I ain't been able to figure. How'd he know?"

Slocum leaned back thoughtfully. When Hook and his bunch, he remembered, rode past him on the ridge, he had felt at the time that Hook was headed somewhere. He had looked it. So, he was headed for the O'Neill place with robbery in mind. Somehow he'd learned about the cache of money and came up to jump claim it. And, by good luck, Jamie and his sister Cathy were elsewhere, tending to the birth of a calf at the time. Otherwise Hook might have wiped out Jamie, and God knows what the bunch would have done to Cathy.

Hook didn't expect to be followed and, funny thing, he didn't seem anxious to wipe out the surviving O'Neills. They didn't kill Jamie when they had the chance. And Cathy was killed only because she had a gun and Hook's own life, at that moment, was in danger.

So what did it add up to?

Slocum stroked his chin. It added up to something other than plain robbery.

John O'Neill, the father, didn't seem to offer resistance, yet he was shot in the face—a sadistic act. The kid, Johnny, was killed because he tried for a gun. The other two O'Neills, Cathy and her brother, were left unharmed.

Why?

It was puzzling, and there was no way yet to get an answer, not till they caught up with Hook Fulton and his bunch. What about the bunch? There were at least four now that Gleason and Baker were gone.

They were a gang of scum and they'd done dirty deeds in Texas and Arizona and, though Slocum was not a lawman, he'd do what he could to bring them to justice.

It wouldn't be easy. They were hard, dangerous killers. Chances were they'd stay only in small lawless towns, where thieves, derelicts, and desperadoes gathered to escape the law. The one law would be the gun.

He glanced at Jamie. The kid drew his Colt like lightning and was a dead shot. Even so, the odds would be with Hook Fulton.

Slocum hitched his belt. They needed not only the fast gun, but all the cunning in the world, to come out on top.

3

They rode slowly down Main Street, over red dirt, eyes alert, gun hands ready. No way to know, Slocum thought, if Hook was in Twisted Fork, but it was best to be ready. Once before, with Gleason and Baker, Hook had tried to ambush; he'd rather use a trick than face an opponent head-on. Slocum kept that in mind.

They walked the horses past Dixon's General Store and Halligan's Livery until they reached Casey's Saloon, then swung off the horses and tied them to the post.

Cowboys and drifters loafed on the porch, and one old-timer on a rickety chair whittled a stick. Their eyes were curious, and Slocum, scanning them, did not recognize any of the Fulton bunch.

Then the batwing doors swung open and two cowboys swaggered out, beefy, belted, spurred, their faces flushed with drink.

One cowboy with black shoe-button eyes and a pudding nose in a square face stared hard at Jamie. He glanced at Jamie's horse, stared again at Jamie, and his mouth, a hard slit, widened in a smile. "Lookit that fierce cowboy, Bart. Sure looks ferocious, sportin' that big shiny pistol."

"Yeah, Carmine, he looks tough enough to chew

nails if you crossed him," Bart said.

Though the words were offensive, the men on the porch couldn't help smiling. Even Slocum found it amusing, because Jamie, slender, handsome, and boyish, looked anything but tough. But his gun, hung low on his belt, looked tough. Slocum felt the words were offensive, even though spoke by a drunk, and called for a square-off. The men on the porch expected it, too, for they leaned forward, intent on what promised to be fun on a dull afternoon in Twisted Fork. But Jamie was not a man for fighting; more for shooting, Slocum thought. His face was composed and, after a quick glance at the cowboys, he no longer looked at them.

"Maybe I ought to cross him," said Carmine with a smirk, "just to see how tough he is." He stepped in front of Jamie, blocking him.

The nerve of these two men astonished Slocum. They were boozed up, yes, and the Kid looked like a tenderfoot, but to throw insult like that for no cause had to bring on sudden grief. A glance convinced Slocum that Jamie would not draw against these hyenas; he'd go against nobody but Hook. Slocum didn't like it. There was something odd in the way these cowboys came out. He'd try to focus their attention.

"Why don't you be nice guys and just go back to guzzling at the bar and keep outa trouble," he said gently.

The men digested his words in silence. Then Carmine's pudding nose twisted in his square face and he glared at Slocum.

"*Who's* gonna give us trouble? The killer kid or just plain you?"

Slocum squinted, but stayed genial. "Again I say, why don't you back off, cowboy. Leave us alone and everyone will be sleeping whole tonight."

Carmine shrugged; he was sticking hard. "And, like I said, who's gonna give trouble? The kid or just plain you?"

"Just plain me," he said. "Because if the Kid pulled his gun, you'd be fulla holes before you reached your holster." He shifted to face them.

Carmine and Bart stared, clearly amazed at his nerve. They glanced at the men on the porch, watching, their eyes shining. Then looked at each other, burst out laughing, and Slocum, hawk-eyed, who knew a diversion when he saw it, watched their hands start downward.

"Kid!" His voice was sharp as his own hand, a lightning blur, moved, and his two shots sounded like one, the bullets tearing through the men, knocking them back as if they'd been poleaxed. They dropped.

Slocum's eyes slid to the porch. Everyone was frozen, staring at the fallen men. He, too, looked at them. They'd been a plant, of course—gunmen recruited by Fulton to pick a fight and wipe them out. He drew a breath, slipped his gun back to its holster, and turned to Jamie.

The Kid hadn't even drawn.

Later, standing at the bar, they nursed a couple of whiskeys. The saloon was spacious, with men playing cards at two tables, and three women loafing near some men.

Slocum studied the drinkers—a motley collection, but none in the Fulton bunch. They looked back at him curiously, but nobody talked. Slocum turned to the barkeep, Casey, a short, pink-faced man with his hair parted in the middle and plastered down. His voice was low. "Could I ask if Hook Fulton passed through here?"

Casey's face was careful. He nodded, polished a glass.

"Say where he was headed?"

Casey smiled. "Hook Fulton never says where he's headed."

It was a dumb question, Slocum knew, but it had to be asked. "Gimme another whiskey," he said. Jamie still nursed his first drink.

Casey filled the glass. "That was fancy shootin' out there, mister. I heard about it."

"The name's Slocum. Those men came out to start a fight. Who were they?"

Casey's light blue eyes stayed steady on his, then he shrugged. "Carmine and Bart, a couple of gunmen from Phoenix. Rough boys. You put 'em outa their misery."

Slocum's jaw was hard. "Hired guns?"

Casey's smile was noncommittal.

Slocum looked at the women. "Hook's a ladies' man. Did he favor one of the girls?"

Casey's lids slid down. "He talked to Rosalie. It's all I know. She's in the red dress."

Slocum looked at her, a buxom redhead with heavy breasts and plenty of hip. She was talking with a girl at the other end of the saloon. Slocum felt a tingle in his loins. He could use some rip-roaring sex, and this Rosalie looked tempting.

Jamie spoke up. "Let's shove along, Slocum."

Slocum turned to stare at him. His handsome face looked sour, as if he didn't like what was happening.

"Hang in there, Kid. Maybe I can find out something from the woman."

"Just wasting time. Let's move."

Slocum scowled, studied the Kid's tight-lipped face.

"Why in hell didn't you draw out there? I warned you."

The Kid's blue eyes glittered oddly. "I'm sorry. I didn't dream they would draw."

"They wanted a fight. Couldn't you read it?"

"I knew they wanted it, but hoped to bypass them. It's Hook Fulton who killed my family. I'm not gonna stop for every nickel-and-dime gunman who likes a shootout."

Slocum shook his head. In a way, the Kid was right, but not *all* right. "These men wanted to stop us. I can understand you wanting to stick with Fulton, but if someone's out to mow you down, you gotta defend yourself."

Jamie bit his lip, as if annoyed at the discussion. "Yeah, yeah, but we gotta try and stick to the target, Hook Fulton. We gotta get around these tinhorn gunmen out to prove how good they are."

Slocum nodded; the Kid made a good case, but with a hyena like Carmine, you couldn't avoid a showdown.

Rosalie had turned and was looking at him as if she sensed he was a male animal primed for sex. He started toward her.

"Where the hell you goin'?" the Kid demanded.

"Just sit tight while I check out a few things, Jamie."

As Slocum walked toward Rosalie, he couldn't

help smiling at the disgusted look on the Kid's face.
He hated the idea of a woman slowing down the pursuit of Hook Fulton, no doubt.

"Howdy," he said. "Slocum's the name. John Slocum." She smiled, showing white, even teeth; she had
a full lower lip and her gray eyes were flecked with
green. "You're a good-looking man, Slocum."

"You're not so bad," he grinned. Her breasts came
out like swollen, pointed pears, the nipples pressing
hard against the silk of her thin red dress. She had a
well-fleshed body, ripe and ready. Again he felt tingles
in his loins. Her female instinct picked up his feelings.

"What's your pleasure, Slocum?"

His eyes traveled over the buxom body and he
grinned. "Whiskey and you look like a man's idea of
pleasure."

A dreamy look came to the gray eyes, and a slow
smile twisted her lips. "Just follow me, Slocum; I
know where you can get both."

The stairs in the back of the saloon led to a room
with a window facing Main Street. It had a double
bed with a green coverlet, a wooden table, two chairs,
a bottle of whiskey, and two glasses.

She poured the whiskey into the glasses. "Haven't
seen you in these parts, Slocum. Where you from?"

He smiled grimly. "From a lotta parts, Rosalie. A
well-traveled man." He drank the whiskey. "You look
like a well-traveled woman."

"I'm from the Oklahoma Territory."

He lifted his glass again, his green eyes piercing.
"Hook Fulton came outa Oklahoma."

She frowned. "Are you a lawman, Slocum?"

He smiled. "Not me. Just an ordinary cowboy ambling through town."

"You don't look ordinary to me." She sipped her drink. "Funny thing. Hook rode through here just a while back. Friend of yours, maybe?"

"I played poker with him and won some of his money. Figure he'd like another game."

She smiled. "Hook Fulton doesn't like to lose nothin', especially money."

"Say where he's headed?" Slocum kept his tone casual.

Her eyes narrowed. "Looks like you came up here to talk about Hook Fulton. I'm not in the business of gossiping."

Slocum's jaw hardened. "Listen, Miss Bellybutton. Hook Fulton is a drinking man, a ladies' man, and a killing man. Now, I figure he talked a lot to you during his drinking. So why don't you tell me where he's headed?"

Her mouth grew tight. "You're no friend of Hook's. And you came up here on false pretenses."

Slocum pulled a gleaming golden eagle, put it on the table. "No. I'm here because you're a whole lot of woman. But Hook's been throwing a lot of lead. He's got to pay."

She picked up the coin. "You're a mighty generous man, Mr. Slocum. Nothing would give me more pleasure than to pleasure you. But I'd like to warn you. Hook Fulton is smart as the devil. Nobody's ever put a finger on him in years of rustlin', robbin', and killin'. You're biting off more than you can chew, if you go against him." She poured another whiskey. "He's not goin' to tell a girl like me where he's goin'. He stays alive because he doesn't trust anyone."

Slocum heaved a sigh and lifted his glass. It had to be true; Hook Fulton seemed to lead a charmed life. He was wanted in three states for killing and robbing, yet nobody ever laid a hand on him. He was one of those outlaws who could smell danger and moved right to save his hide. He gathered thieves and desperadoes around him, and when lead got thrown, it was they who went down, never Hook. Yes, he was too smart to trust anyone.

He looked at Rosalie, at her buxom body, and his expression made her smile. "Why bother your head about Hook at a time like this?" she said.

Slocum grinned. That thought hit him, too. She was a great piece of woman, with those swollen breasts. She put her full-lipped mouth up for kissing and pressed her breasts against him. He felt the jump in his jeans. She must have felt it, too, for she muttered, "Slocum, you are primed for love." She pulled her dress over her head, pulled off her chemise and stood there, the nipples of her breasts pointing at him. Her waist was slender, her hips wide, her legs well-shaped. He started, but she said, "Maybe you better get your duds off first, Slocum."

He drew a heavy breath, pulled them off fast, and her eyes gleamed at the sight of his male excitement. He moved to her; her breasts were smooth as silk, the bulge of them mouth-filling. He tongued her nipples and she cooed with pleasure. His hand went down into the velvet moisture and played. She heaved a sigh. She reached for his bristling flesh and caressed it while he stroked her. She slid down and brought him to her lips. She was clever and gave him great pleasure. Then she pulled him to the bed and he slipped

into her, his bigness filling her, and plunged deep.
She moaned at the impact. He moved on her, his hands
on her breasts and her buttocks, while his hips thrust,
again and again, and the pleasure kept rising and rising. Her body would tighten, and she'd grab him in
a vise-like grip. Then he grabbed her buttocks and
began to plunge hard, repeatedly, as the searing, soaring pleasure went through him.

She moaned, and her body coiled with pleasure.
They lay there in silence for a time.

Then she said, "Slocum, after that I doubt if I could
hold anything back from you. Hook Fulton said enough
for me to believe he's riding south. Could be Santa
Fe."

When he came downstairs, he saw Jamie at the table,
nursing a drink. His blue eyes burned hard. "Well?"

Slocum shrugged. "Well, what?"

"You put in a lot of good time up there. I hope it
was worth it." Jamie's voice rasped.

Slocum had to smile. "It was worth it, Kid. Isn't
it about time you found out?"

The lids slid for a moment, and when they came
up, the eyes were fierce. "Found out what?"

Slocum pulled a havana and scuffed his finger-
nail on a lucifer. " 'Bout the pleasures of women," he
said casually.

Jamie's teeth clenched. "Slocum, you're something
of a pig, playing around with that sow. Wasting time.
We're supposed to be hunting down Hook Fulton, not
jumping into bed with shady ladies."

Slocum stared, astonished. *Hell's fire*, he thought,
this young stud is one stick-in-the-mud. It had to be
his youth.

"Well, young fella, you don't know much about women, I can see that. Ain't learned to like them yet, have you? But I'll tell you a secret. If a woman likes you, she gives you everything. Now, I found out that Hook is headed south."

Jamie threw him a disgusted look. "But we know that."

"He's not only going south, but probably to Santa Fe."

Jamie tightened his gunbelt and his jaw clenched. "Let's go."

Slocum, drink in hand, watched Jamie start for the door. The Kid wasn't going to waste a moment in his effort to trap and mow down Hook Fulton. Yet something looked comic in the way Jamie's young slender body moved, hunched and determined. That was how it seemed to strike a red-faced cowboy sitting at a nearby table with a glass in his hand. He smirked and, in mischief, stuck out his booted leg, tripping Jamie, which sent him toward the floor. But as the Kid hit it, he turned. His gun was suddenly in hand and there was the crack of gunfire and the splintering of glass as the drink spattered. The red-faced cowboy's eyes were wide in shock as he stared at the tenderfoot on the floor, still holding his gun.

Slocum, grim-faced, had come to his feet and walked to the man, pulling him to his feet.

"You must be daft in the head. Don't know how close you come to getting yourself scattered over the table."

The man's face looked more white than red as he ambled over, mumbling something to Jamie. He put out his hand to pull him up. "I'm sorry, pardner. Must have gone loco. Don't know what made me do it.

Thought it'd be funny, but it wasn't."

Jamie scowled, slipped the gun back into its holster. "Forget it," he said, tight-lipped.

The jasper wiped his mouth nervously. "Damn it, cowboy, you remind me of Billy the Kid. I saw him once in Kansas City. He pulled the fastest gun I ever saw. Like you."

Slocum couldn't help smiling as he saw respect in the eyes of the men in the saloon. If Jamie, when he came to a town, were to pull his gun one time, he'd get all the respect he wanted. Because Jamie looked so boyish, bewhiskered men in tough little towns found it hard to take him seriously.

They walked out to the hitch rack, where they swung over their saddles and rode down the dusty street. Some men came out to the porch, looking after them. Slocum, aware of the sort of things that can happen when a man's back is turned, glanced around. The red-faced cowboy was standing with the others, and if he had hostile intent, it wasn't showing. His gun was holstered, and he just shook his head, as if it had hit him for the first time that he had almost booted himself into eternity.

4

As they rode, Slocum glanced at Jamie, the way he sat, erect in the saddle, the easy way he handled his black. Slocum smiled, thinking the Kid was a bundle of contradictions; he looked soft, but he could shoot out a snake's eyes; he rode smart, but in the bar he had looked like a tenderfoot. No wonder that cowboy clown felt he could trip Jamie and get away with it.

Slocum laughed at the memory of the cowboy's face back in the saloon, his shock at the speed with which Jamie had shot the glass from his hand. It was trick shooting, for he'd done it almost as he hit the floor. Jamie was fast, he was sinewy, and his timing quick.

"Hey, Kid."

Jamie looked at him.

"Why do you s'pose that hyena tripped you like that?"

Jamie shot him a shrewd look. "Why do *you* s'pose?"

"Dunno. Musta had a reason."

"The reason was he's a goddamn mulebrain."

"C'mon, now, Jamie. He picked on *you*, he didn't pick on me."

Jamie's mouth was a hard line. "He's a yellowbelly,

36

that's why. There's always a yellowbelly who likes to pick on a small guy. He figures it's safe; figures to get some laughs. But it ain't all that safe. He was just a hair's-breadth away from getting plastered on the wall."

Slocum laughed. "That's right. You held back real good."

Jamie's face was hard. "I don't aim to shoot some mulebrain and start up trouble. We're on a quest to destroy the men who destroyed my family. That's why I didn't pick off that yellowbelly back there."

"Smart move, Jamie," Slocum said, as his eyes raked the Rawhide Mountain.

Black Rock was a small town with ramshackle houses and a red dirt main street with a saloon and some rundown stores. The men in it, as Slocum had expected, looked like a rat pack of thieves and renegade outlaws. The sort of town where Hook might stop to rest and take provisions. Slocum felt it would be smart to do the same and recharge his energies.

As he and Jamie walked their horses down the street, two men came stumbling out of the saloon, cursing each other. After them five men spilled onto the porch, eager to watch something that seemed to be shaping up to a showdown.

One of the two men, Slocum guessed, had said the wrong thing, and now they were on a parched red dirt street in a nowhere town under a scalded sky, ready to shoot each other to hell.

"I'd like all the folks here," said one man, who had a scarred mouth, "to know that I didn't ask for this. Luther insulted me. He gave me no choice but to call him out." He had black shoe-button eyes, and the scar gave his face a sinister look.

Slocum's gaze swung to Luther, a short, stocky man, a bit gnarled, with a rough-lined face and blue eyes clouded by time. "Insult you, Scarbone? Why, every God-fearing man knows you for what you are, a mangy, money-grubbing polecat who'd steal the copper pennies off a dead man's eyes." Luther's voice, excited by his sense of injustice, came out in a screech.

Slocum, sizing up the opponents, felt that Luther had more guts than brains, and that his mouth had just ruined him.

Even Jamie could see it and, though up to now he had wanted no part of anyone's fight other than his own, he seemed to be bothered by this one.

"Can't we stop this?" he muttered to Slocum as they tied the horses to the post.

Slocum shot him a warning look. "Ain't our business."

Scarbone's twisted mouth smiled, not a pretty sight. "Luther, you're arthritic, your fingers and your brain. I'd ask you to 'pologize, 'cept I know you're dumber than an army mule. But I'll give you that chance afore these men to say you're sorry for what you called me."

Luther's anger made his face look purplish. "What I called you is what you are. There's got to be no harm in tellin' the truth. An ornery lowlife who's run with outlaws and who's thieved his way clear across Texas."

A lot of harm in telling the truth, Slocum thought as silence hit the street like a thunderbolt. Everyone froze, aware that words like those could have but one climax.

And it came as both men went for their holsters,

but only one gun spit fire, and Luther seemed lifted off the ground by the bullet that slammed into him. He was dead before he hit the ground.

Scarbone gazed stone-faced at the body, then turned to the onlookers. "I warned him, didn't I?" He blew at the barrel of the gun as if to cool it, and slipped it into his holster. The knife scar at his grinning mouth looked red.

"It was murder," Slocum said softly to Jamie. The Kid just looked venomously at Scarbone.

Though Slocum's voice had been soft, Scarbone turned to scrutinize him, then to look at Jamie. His thin slit of a mouth spread in its strange cruel smile. Slocum stared directly into the black eyes, then turned and went into the saloon, followed by the Kid.

The saloon was big and square, but no surprise, because it was where the life of the town took place. The long bar with a mirror behind it ran perpendicular to the door, and there were six tables for the card players. The players had rushed out to enjoy the entertainment event of the afternoon and were now filing back, talking as they took their seats.

The bartender, a tall, narrow-shouldered man with a cavernous face, came over. "What'll it be, gents?"

"Whiskey," Slocum said. Though he ordered it, he knew Jamie had little taste for drinking. He didn't smoke, drank little, did no whoring. But he did two things well: rode a horse and handled a gun. Slocum wondered how he got to be so good. His moves had been dazzling, and he could probably shoot the eyes out of a rattlesnake at fifty yards. But he didn't pick fights, not like the Colorado Kid, who was fast, young, and wanted a rep. Slocum remembered: he got a rep, but also a bullet in the back. The gossip had been that the Kid had sworn he'd kill Fulton the next time he met him. But the Kid never met Fulton, not face to face. Abe Loomis once told some men he'd seen Fulton shoot Colorado from an upstairs window. Loomis disappeared one night, probably cut down by one of the Fulton gang, so it didn't matter.

As Slocum saw it, the key point was that Fulton, a sly devil, would use a gun only when he had the odds.

Slocum studied the barkeep, his sunken cheeks, thin mouth, and cool brown eyes. Not the sort of man who'd talk loosely. He'd say, "Yeah, Hook Fulton went through," and that would be it.

Slocum lifted his drink and turned to Jamie. In spite of roughing it, the Kid managed to look fresh, his unlined face bronzed by the sun. Hidden fire lurked in the depths of his cobalt-blue eyes, and his thick yellow hair peeped from under his short black hat. His lips were pressed hard, and there was no doubt that only one idea burned in his mind: revenge.

If Jamie had his way, they'd be riding at night, running the horses into the ground to catch up with Fulton. No point to it. The horses had to rest.

Slocum figured he would relax here and that, first thing at dawn, they'd start after Fulton.

"How much time we goin' to spend here?" asked Jamie, gazing at the men in the saloon, then scowling because none of them seemed to belong to the Fulton bunch.

"We're going to rest the horses and eat a good hot meal. We'll start at daybreak."

"You keep thinking of the horses instead of Fulton," Jamie complained.

"It's the horses that are going to bring us to Fulton,

if we don't cripple them first," Slocum said, his voice stern. While he understood Jamie's craving for revenge, he didn't go for the idea of killing the horses trying.

In the mirror behind the bar he saw Scarbone swagger in, bristling a bit, as if daring anyone to challenge what he'd just done: shot down a crotchety old-timer. He glanced at Jamie and seemed amused, but said nothing, then sauntered to the card table where four ratty-looking players smiled, as if he'd done something heroic out on the street.

"I hated to shoot Luther," Scarbone said, "but he bad-mouthed me, as you all heard. Jest because a man's got gray hair don't give him the right to run his mouth loose."

"Yuh, right, Scarbone," said a man with a pouchy face, speaking in a hoarse whiskey voice. He wore a yellow vest and a watch chain. "Luther yapped too much. Jest because yuh once rode with the Fulton bunch didn't give Luther the right to bad-mouth yuh. Luther was dumb as an army mule. Didn't know when to shut up."

"There's more than one like that," said Scarbone, throwing a glance at Slocum. He sat at the table. "Let's play poker."

Jamie's mouth was a hard line. "Did you hear that?" he said in a low voice to Slocum. The Kid was seething.

"Keep a lid on it," Slocum said. "He had nothing to do with your family."

Jamie's eyes blazed. "I hate the sight of that Scarbone. Not only because he rode with Hook, but the way he killed that old man."

Slocum turned sharply. The Kid was in a rage,

ready to go off half-cocked. He had no real beef against Scarbone. Though he once rode with Fulton, he didn't ride against Jamie's family. He was getting it all mixed up in his head. Probably he was thinking Luther was like his own father, gunned down by a cold-blooded killer.

"Go slow, Kid. This man did nothing to you."

Jamie took a deep breath, sipped at the whiskey, as if trying to simmer down. "He's rotten, and he's rode with Fulton. It means he's done the same kind of killin'."

"Yeah, but he's done nothing to you. Keep that in mind. We can't go out and clean up the world. Seems smart to save yourself for Fulton."

Jamie's lips pressed. "Guess you're right."

Slocum put his elbows on the bar and switched the subject. "Hey, Kid, I always meant to ask. How in hell did you get to shoot like that? And draw that fast?"

Jamie turned slowly to face him, and for the first time a grin appeared on his face. "You mean that?"

Slocum nodded. "Wouldn't say it if I didn't."

The grin disappeared. "It was Dad. He had us shootin' all the time—me, Cathy, Johnny. Knocking off bottles, hittin' all sorts of small targets. Practicing drawing fast and shootin' fast. Wanted us to be the best. Said it over and over—to protect yourself in this country, you gotta draw fast and shoot straight. There's a lot of mangy dogs out there who want to do you dirt." Jamie's eyes misted. "Dad was right. The trouble was, he didn't have a gun and a chance to follow his own advice, when the Fulton bunch came down on him."

Slocum nodded thoughtfully. Odd how the old man,

O'Neill, had insisted all the kids learn to shoot, even the girl, Cathy. What was he afraid of? Another piece of the puzzle. How in hell did he get all that money, big money? Gold prospecting? Maybe he didn't get it legally. Anything was possible.

Anyway, it explained why Jamie could shoot so fast and straight. Slocum raised his glass, thinking. Up to now, Jamie hadn't pulled his gun in a one-on-one. He seemed to be saving himself for Fulton. But somehow, the way Scarbone shot Luther put Jamie in mind of how his own father died. He seemed ready to take on Scarbone for his father's death. Didn't make much sense. Scarbone was a hyena, but he'd done nothing to them, and it'd be right foolish to waste a bullet on him.

"Hey, boy."

It was Scarbone, and he was looking at Jamie.

Jamie turned slowly, as did Slocum.

Scarbone was grinning. "Figure you might want to play some poker. Am I right?"

Jamie's eyes began to glitter. "I don't play poker, mister."

Scarbone's grin began to broaden. "What game do you play?"

Everyone in the bar quieted down to watch.

"I don't play cards," Jamie said coldly.

Scarbone glanced at the men at his table. "I take it yore daddy didn't want you to get into bad habits."

The rat pack around him laughed.

"I'll play poker with you, Scarbone," Slocum said, coming forward.

The smile vanished, and a sullen look appeared on Scarbone's lean face. "Sure, sure. Sit down. Make room, men. What's the handle, mister?"

"Slocum. John Slocum."

Scarbone's eyes narrowed. "Seems like I heard the name, up in Kansas."

"I been there," Slocum said flatly, sitting down.

Scarbone's look was crafty. "Don't exactly know where I heard it. You a wanted man? In trouble with the law?"

Slocum smiled grimly. "Would it make any difference?" Jamie had taken a position behind Slocum, facing Scarbone.

"Not a bit of difference," grinned Scarbone. "We're an easy-goin' bunch of men in this town. Nobody is lily-white. It's just a bit peculiar."

"What is?"

"Seeing a man like you traveling with this tenderfoot."

Slocum's green eyes drilled hard at Scarbone. "What's that mean?"

"You got the look...well, of a man of experience," Scarbone said. "Wouldn't expect you to have a saddle buddy like him, a tenderfoot."

There was dead silence. Slocum shook his head. "You like to live dangerously, Scarbone. The way I see it, you just shot an old man with a rusty draw. Now you aim to tangle with a tenderfoot. I'd like to warn you that this tenderfoot can shoot out both your eyes before you got your gun out." He laughed. "But I don't let him shoot, 'cause I like a fair fight."

The men listened with amazement. Only the fact that it was told with a solemn face by a formidable man like Slocum kept them from laughing. They gazed at Jamie, at his slender build, at his clear boyish skin, and it was clear they didn't believe Slocum. But they felt he was not a man to be trifled with, so they kept straight faces.

Scarbone, too, seemed less interested in Jamie than in Slocum, who he felt would be a rough man to tangle with. He heartily disliked what Slocum had said, and the contempt in his voice, but he wasn't ready to make a move. Not now. Two dark spots burned in his cheek as he said, "You wanted to play poker. Let's play." He started to deal and the tension at the table went down.

They began to play. Slocum noticed the stakes were not high. Nobody would get rich through gambling. Scarbone seemed to take pride in his play, and figured it might be fun to humiliate the stranger who'd come in with this yearling and talked so big. He had heard Slocum's comment to Jamie, after the shootout with Luther, that it had been murder. In Scarbone's mind, Slocum had said things that couldn't be swallowed. A man could hardly hold up his head if he took stuff like that. As for that tenderfoot shooting like Lightnin' Joe, that had to be a cock-and-bull story. He was just a pretty boy, a rosy-cheeked colt, who tried to look tough as nails.

Scarbone began to sweat hard to make Slocum look like a chump at cards. But it was one of those days when, no matter what cards he held, good or bad, Slocum's were just a bit better. It riled him, made him wonder if Slocum was a shark. Scarbone's jaw hardened. He had to take Slocum on; it was a matter of pride. He glanced at the man's rugged face, the piercing green eyes that seemed to drill through you. He had the kind of look that made you think twice about calling him out.

"Where you fellas ridin' in from," asked the man in the yellow vest, who was called Dutch.

"From East Texas," Slocum said.

"See anything of Apaches? Heard tell they're kickin' up hell."

"They're doin' that, all right," Slocum said.

The men at the table and nearby, grim-faced, turned to him.

"What happened?" asked Scarbone.

"They staked out a couple of men in the hot sun. By the time we got there, the big ants had done the job," Slocum said.

There was a long silence.

"Who were the men? Did you know them?" Dutch asked.

"Yeah, I knew them. They used to run with Hook Fulton—Gleason and Baker."

"Poor Gleason," said Scarbone, and he looked pale.

Nobody played cards, and there was silence.

"I understand you used to ride with Hook Fulton in the old days," said Jamie.

Everyone turned to look at him. It was the first time he'd opened up, and his young voice contrasted with the guttural voices of the other men.

Scarbone grinned. "Yeah, young fella, I rode with him." He laughed insolently. "Maybe you're a lawman, gonna carry me off to the pen." Everyone laughed.

Jamie's teeth clenched. "Men who ride with Hook don't belong in the pen. They belong six feet under."

Slocum was astounded. The Kid, standing there watching Scarbone, had just gone loco. He had shifted, facing Scarbone. Slocum went taut, his eyes hawk-like, watching. He caught the glance Scarbone slipped

Dutch. Slocum felt he should head things off. The setup looked wrong. He didn't know how Jamie would handle a showdown. He'd never done it, and he might falter just a whisper at the thought of killing, which would get him dead. Slocum had to head it off.

"Just a minute," he began, but it was already too late.

"This ain't your business," Scarbone snarled, and turned to Jamie. "You're a sawed-off squirt with a bad mouth. Luther talked wrong, too. You saw what happened to him."

Jamie was too far gone now, Slocum could see; there was no stopping him. His lip curled with contempt. "You shot an old man with a rusty arm. You figure it makes you a big man. It makes you a gutless yellowbelly."

The silence was overwhelming. Rage made Scarbone's face flame, and his mouth twisted horribly. He stood. "Draw, you little bastard," he hissed, and his hand shot down to his gun. He was fast. He got it free of the holster when Jamie's bullet slammed into his chest, and he went down squirming. At the same time, Slocum had his gun out, pointing it at Dutch, who was trying for his holster and froze.

The men looked down at Scarbone, then at Jamie. One of the men swore softly. "Did you see that draw? Holy mother!"

Slocum spoke to Dutch. "Toss your gun here, and be careful." Slocum shook out the bullets and put the gun on the table. "Don't reload," he said grimly. He let his eyes drift over the others, and what he saw seemed to satisfy him.

He jerked his head to the door. Jamie calmly slipped his Colt into its oiled holster and, with a last glance

at Scarbone, walked from the saloon out to the hitch
rack. Slocum pulled a havana and fired a match. He
puffed at the cigar and grinned.

"Looks like the Kid cleaned up your town a bit,"
he said. As he walked through the batwing doors, he
noticed a few smiles.

They rode in silence. The land looked lonely under a
red and purple sky. The sun dipped behind the great
mountain ranges to the west.

Slocum began to look for a campsite, and with a
bit of disgust realized they'd have to eat jerky instead
of the hot stew he'd been counting on.

"What in hell made you go for Scarbone like that?"
he demanded.

Jamie, who had been grim-faced, now looked
cheerful. "'Cause he was a no-good, slimy rat, that's
why."

Slocum shook his head. The description was right,
but Scarbone had done nothing to Jamie. Well, he had
been insulting. But Scarbone still had done nothing
to hurt Jamie, and it was a bit hard to understand why
Jamie had risked a shootout with a dangerous outlaw.

Jamie stared at the mountain ranges, as if hoping
to spot his real enemy, Fulton. He spoke slowly. "Scarbone was a killer. He rode with Hook Fulton once.
Probably killed men like my father. You saw how he
killed Luther, that old man, like you'd squash a bug.
And those oily words afterward, like it hurt him more.
It was murder. You said it first, Slocum."

Slocum shrugged: the Kid was in a killing mood
since he had lost his family, and Scarbone was the
nearest thing to Hook. Jamie had to act, or all the

poison inside him would explode. That was how Slocum figured it.

Well, Scarbone's death was no great loss. He was
a thieving outlaw whose career in stealing and killing
had been brought to a screeching halt.

The Kid deserved a cheer, not a grumble.

5

They rode to a grove of cottonwoods and Slocum studied the land. Nothing threatening, a good place to camp, to clean up, get the grime off his body, and cool down the horses. He'd seen a couple of coyotes quarreling over a rabbit, and figured he'd find one in the thickets near the stream.

"We'll camp here," he said. Jamie shrugged. He didn't seem to care where they camped, looked at all stops as a necessary evil. To him, the one problem was not to lose time, so they would not lose Hook.

A jackrabbit streaked across the edge of Slocum's vision and he fired. The rabbit jumped and fell. "Fresh meat for dinner," Slocum grinned.

After he retrieved the rabbit, he pulled off his shirt. "Let's get in the water and wash some of the dirt off."

Jamie rubbed his chin. "You go ahead. I'll dig a hole, get a fire started."

Slocum scowled. "Are you gonna bathe, or you gonna stink like a buffalo?"

Jamie grinned. "It's you who do the stinkin' 'round here. You sweat like a buffalo. I don't sweat."

Slocum shook his head. It was true. Somehow the Kid seemed to stay neat, no matter what they went through.

"I'll wash up later," Jamie said, digging the pans out of the saddlebag. The Kid had a sense of modesty; he was young, Slocum thought. He threw his duds on the ground near the stream and jumped in. The cool water hit his hot body with a pleasant shock. He thrashed around, scrubbed his body, then came out to lie on the grass near his gun. He was a man who hated to be far from his gun at any time. His eyes swept the surrounding land as he slipped into his clothes. He could see the far-off mountain range, still brilliant in the sun, the swale, the cottonwoods, the brush, the thistleweeds, and the curve of the stream. He listened quietly, aware of a feeling of unease. He could hear Jamie moving about, the horses cropping quietly. Again his eyes swept the surrounding land, but he could see nothing. He turned to Jamie. "Get in the water, Kid."

Jamie nodded and started for the stream. The rabbit was roasting on the spit over the fire, and already sent out an appetizing scent. Slocum put some beans on a pan and pushed them around as they heated.

He glanced back at the stream, looking for Jamie, but couldn't see him. He was one modest fellow, probably had gone a bit upstream, around the curve, to bathe. He put the coffee pot on the fire, then stopped to listen. Something wasn't right.

Slocum glanced at the horses. The roan's ears were perked. A shot of tension went through Slocum. He turned his head slowly and his hand moved to his holster. His instinct was right. Some animal, or something more sinister, was nearby. Where the hell was Jamie? His piercing green eyes scanned the brush, the cottonwoods. He crouched and, moving low, went toward the stream. He followed Jamie's tracks, moving upstream, around the curve. Then he saw the moccasin tracks. Apache—one. A scuffle here, a silent one. The Apache had grabbed Jamie. But why hadn't he tomahawked him? Knifed him? Why grab him? Every muscle in Slocum's body was taut as he strained his ears to listen. In the thicket to his left, the silence was overwhelming, not even a bird or insect sound. He moved like a cat, silently, straining his eyes to see through the sagebrush. Something on the ground—a white figure. Dead? It jolted him, his concentration, but still he heard the whisper of movement, and instinct made him turn to see the muscled Apache, brown eyes glaring, mouth twisted with hatred, his arm coming down with the tomahawk. Slocum's powerful arm shot up, caught the Apache's wrist, held it, caught his other hand that went for the throat. They fell, rolled over and over, the Apache on top, Slocum pinned sideways. But Slocum held hard to the wrist and, with a ferocious wrench, twisted it, heard the Apache groan as the bone snapped, and the tomahawk fell from the dead fingers. The Apache instantly butted his head against Slocum's, stunning him long enough for the Indian to grab his knife and bring it up for the plunge.

Again Slocum's arm shot up, holding the arm, and they stared at each other. Slocum realized it was the fourth Apache, the one who got away, who kept tracking, determined to avenge the deaths of his tribesmen. It showed in his hate-filled, glaring eyes. The veins of his neck swelled as he strained to bring down the deadly blade while Slocum held him fixed. They froze like that until the Apache, because of his superior position, began to inch the knife closer. Slocum's gun was pinned under the side of his body. He was close to death, inches away, and Slocum, with desperate urgency, jerked violently, which shifted his body. Lightning-quick, his right hand went down to his gun, and the bullet crashed into the Apache's body, which jumped at the impact. Like an empty sack, he slid off Slocum's body, and the glaring eyes went empty.

Slocum lay motionless, pulling deep breaths of air into his lungs. Strength came slowly back to his body. He glanced at the Apache. Even in death he looked powerful: a big chest, a square, blunt face, bronze skin, and the red kerchief holding his long black hair. One of the four Apaches who had staked Gleason and Baker, and came down howling from the rise after Slocum and Jamie. The one who had wheeled his horse sharply into safety. But he had never stopped tracking them, circling the town, waiting for them on the southwest trail. He found them on this stream, where he made his attack.

Jamie . . . where the hell was he? Was it him, naked and dead up there, behind the sagebrush? Slocum's fierce struggle with the Apache had kept him from thinking of anything else. Now the mystery of Jamie rushed into his mind.

He struggled to his feet, feeling aches and pains, and walked into the thicket. His eyes goggled.

A woman lay there, a startling sight, her white flesh against the earth. A beautiful young thing. Was she dead? No, she was breathing. There was a red gash on the side of her head, where the Apache had hit her. Slocum stared, aware suddenly that she looked familiar, but not completely. The face . . . it looked like that sister of Jamie—the yellow hair, the same face. Slocum's eyes shocked open. Good God, could it be?

Slocum stared in a daze. It was Jamie, even though

the body was female! Young breasts, shapely thighs, blonde hair between them. Oh, she was a woman, all right. He stood still, almost forgetting to breathe. A woman! All this time, Jamie had been a young woman! How in hell did he . . . *she* manage to conceal that? Slocum's mind ran to all the small things that had puzzled him. Her modesty, never bathing with him, the way she nursed her drinks, her jealousy. The way something seemed to tick men off in saloons, made them pick on her. As if they sensed something. Why didn't he pick it up? After all, she was shaped like a young woman, she had curves. It was her clothes— loose-fitting, baggy, they hid her curves. Her hair was boy-cut, and with that hat clamped on her, a boy's loose shirt, the way she swaggered, the way she pulled her gun. A tomboy, she could have fooled anyone.

But why the masquerade?

He leaned over her. She was breathing quietly; would come around soon. He'd dump water on her. He took one more glance as he started for the stream. One beautiful girl.

At the stream, he gathered up her clothing and gunbelt, and filled his hat with water. He covered her body with her shirt so the shock of waking nude in front of him wouldn't hit her too hard, then emptied the water from his hat over her face.

She gasped, stirred, groaned, and, eyes still closed, her hand moved to the gash on her forehead. Then her eyes opened and she saw him.

She looked like someone coming out of a deep sleep. Then she became aware that her face was wet, and her hand went to it, to the shirt on her body. Then came the realization she was practically nude. Then she remembered the Apache and her eyes shut tightly. "Oh, God," she moaned.

Her eyes opened with a snap. "Don't stand there staring, you big ape."

Slocum grinned, shrugged, turned, and walked back to the campsite.

She needed a lot of time to get things right in her head.

He did, too, for that matter.

The meat on the spit was almost scorched. Slocum took it off the fire and cut it into strips. He put the beans back on the fire, stirred them, and poured coffee into two tin cups.

He sipped coffee and settled down to wait. His back and shoulder muscles ached from the strain put on them, and it felt good to sit quietly. The sun had gone past the steep towering peaks of the mountains to the west. The sky took on the orange flame of sunset. His eyes swept the countryside. He could see the squat junipers and desert cedars, some yellow-flowered prickly pear.

His mind went back to Twisted Fork and Rosalie, and he had to smile. At the time he had urged *Jamie* to have a go at Rosalie, and remembered the words she had used, which had startled him. "You're a pig, wasting your time with that sow." He thought the words had been harsh, but now he understood them in a new light. He grinned. But it came down to this: what in hell was he going to do with her? Could he travel with Jamie now that he knew? The Kid was a streak of lightning with that gun. A tough one to figure.

He looked at the sinking sun. She was moving like

molasses. Would she ever come out? Was it modesty?

Then he saw her. But again, she looked like Jamie, a tenderfoot, a good-looking kid with yellow hair. If he hadn't seen her body, he'd never guess her to be a girl. But he knew, and it would be impossible from now on not to think of her as anything but a young woman under those clothes.

When she came out of the sagebrush, her cobalt-blue eyes were hard fixed. Not shy as a violet, but bold as brass; that was her style.

"What's your name? Real name?" he asked.

"Janie."

"Close enough. Sit down; your food's getting cold."

She took up her plate of fried meat and beans and ate with hunger.

"How's the head?" he asked. The bruise was still there, though faded a bit.

"All right. Got a small headache, but it'll pass. He wasn't aiming to kill me. Not for a while." Her voice was dry, and she sipped coffee. "I just got a glimpse when he hit me. I went out, didn't remember a thing." She bit her lip. "But from the way that ground was chewed up, I can imagine the fight that went on while I was sleeping easy. That Apache looked all broken up. Tomahawk, knife. Are you all right, Slocum?"

"Bruised a bit." He stretched his legs. "Well, Janie O'Neill, will you tell me why you are traveling in disguise?"

"It's no mystery. Cathy and me were going after the men who killed our father and brother. The way to do it was like men, not young ladies. I cut my hair, slipped into Dad's cord pants, his shirt. They were loose, which helped. Cathy couldn't fit—too womanly." She stared at him. "Nothing wrong with it. You can't see two women tracking a killer gang in the territory, can you?"

She heaved a sigh, then the fire came into her eyes. "When Hook killed Cathy, I knew I'd never give up, no matter what. It was a blessing when you shot down from the hills. You helped Cathy, she shot that filthy pig on top of her. She tried to get Fulton . . . but . . ." Janie rubbed her eyes and sipped the coffee. "When you offered to help, it was like a prayer answered. Oh, I was going after him, no matter what happened. It'd have been tough, but one way or another I was going to get him. But I thank you for your help. It's great having you along." She smiled. "You just saved me from that Apache. I won't ever forget it."

Slocum couldn't help feel a tug at his emotions. "Janie, you sure got a lot of guts." There was admiration in his voice. "Are you going to wear those pants all the time?"

Her face hardened. "Till Hook or me is dead."

Slocum gazed at her and now, in spite of her clothes, he saw her as a young woman; it would be impossible to think of her any more as anything else. But his feelings about her were different, and the image of her body with its flowing female lines was etched in his mind forever.

No; he could think of her as the Kid, or call her Jamie, but she was a young woman, and that was a fact.

The trail went southwest, and Slocum found Hook Fulton's prints easy to follow. Five horses, two with cracked hoofprints. The sun was sailing high over the vast mountain ranges when they sighted the town of Whistling Rock. When they cantered across the wooden bridge over a narrow stream, Slocum could see dingy buildings down a long street.

Always attentive to the horses, Slocum stopped at the Hollis Livery, where a thick-set, broad-faced man with flat gray eyes looked up from pounding a shoe.

Slocum tried a smile. "Expect to be here a short spell. There's a loose shoe on the roan. Will you grain the horses?"

Hollis nodded. "That'll be a silver dollar."

Slocum gave him two.

Hollis looked at the money.

"Where can we get some eats?" Slocum asked.

"Mrs. Smith's Home-Cooked Meals. She got beef stew."

"Sounds good."

Hollis looked at the roan. "Fine horseflesh."

"The best." Slocum looked at his magnificent lines, the muscular chest, the glowing black eyes, so knowing. He pulled a havana and fired it up. "Happen to see four riders go through town lately?"

Hollis kept studying the roan. "Nope."

Then he turned. Slocum stared into the flat gray eyes; there was nothing there.

"I'm looking for Hook Fulton."

"Ain't seen a thing, mister." He paused. "Want your dollar back?"

Slocum grinned. "What the hell." He turned to Janie. "Looks like Mr. Hollis has learned the secret of a long life."

The broad face grinned. "Yes, sir. See no evil, speak no evil."

"The trouble with that," said Janie, staring hard at the man, "is that evil lives a lot longer than it should."

Hollis considered the slender cowboy in front of

him. "I don't even take offense at what a little rabbit like you says." He smiled affably, seemed loosened up. "I got a wife and kid, and the idea of leaving them a widow and an orphan don't appeal to me." He rubbed the roan's haunches. "I jest take care o' the hosses, keep my mouth shut, and every week I go to church and say a prayer for some poor departed soul who, in anger or greed, pulled his six-shooter."

He patted the roan. "I see no evil, speak no evil; just care for the hosses. I say that if men were more like hosses, we'd all be better off."

Slocum looked grim. "The trouble, Hollis, is that men are not like horses. They're more like wolves. And some need to get their fangs pulled. If we had to depend on men like you, it'd never happen. Let's go, Kid."

He glanced at Hollis as they walked out. His mouth was tight. He didn't like that, Slocum thought. There were always men ready to live with evil. They seemed to think that if they did nothing they wouldn't get hurt. But after the wolf ran out of victims, it turned on its own.

The powdered dust of the street rose with their steps, and they passed Mrs. Smith's Home-Cooked Meals. At Golden's General Store Slocum said, "Reckon you might get some victuals and put them into the saddlebags. I'll check the saloon. Meet me there."

She threw him a cool look and turned to the store.

Slocum smiled. She wasn't crazy about shopping. She could be thinking that, since he'd discovered she was a woman, he was ready to dump woman things on her, like groceries and cooking. Nothing could be further from his mind. Sure, she was a filly, a lovely

one, but she pulled a fast gun, and everything about
her was . . . well . . . red-blooded.

The two-story saloon's sign read: Macreedy—
Liquor, Girls, Rooms. About ten men were scattered
in the saloon, seven at the card tables, three at the
bar. Two girls chatted at the back table.

Slocum scrutinized the men, but it was pointless.
Hook was not stupid, and would hardly leave his men
where they'd be recognized by his pursuers. Slocum
had seen some in Abilene with Fulton, and at the
gunfight with Janie and her sister. He knew that Ironfist Gault and Hank Bacon, a vicious pair, had killed
during a bank robbery in Wichita. He didn't know the
other two men, but he would recognize them. They
were lean, hard-bitten outlaws who looked dangerous
and fast. Slocum had been baffled as to why Fulton
didn't stand and shoot it out. A mystery, but it wasn't
fear. Either he was in a hurry to get somewhere with
the loot stolen from O'Neill, or he wanted an edge
before the fight, or he'd recruit other men to do his
fighting. Slocum kept this in mind as he studied the
faces of the men in the saloon.

The barkeep came over, a smiling, rusty-haired
man with a nose that bore the scars of many a fistfight.
"Macreedy," he said. "What'll it be?"

"Whiskey."

Macreedy put a bottle and a glass in front of him.
His shrewd blue eyes scrutinized Slocum. "Hot day,
mister."

"Slocum's the name. Yeah, it's hot."

He tossed off the drink and Macreedy poured another.

"Where you riding in from, Slocum?"

"East."

"Apaches?"

"Saw four."

Macreedy looked serious. "There's a bunch of them, prowling, hitting pilgrims coming from the east."

A cowboy with a brown Stetson at the bar said, "They're riled up. We ought to get the troops out here."

"Not serious enough for troops," said Macreedy.

Slocum eyed his whiskey. "Get a lotta riders going through?"

Macreedy grinned. "We get plenty. If you're going to Santa Fe, you gotta hit Whistling Rock. We get all sorts."

Slocum lifted his drink. "How long ago did Hook Fulton go through?" he asked.

Macreedy looked thoughtfully at Slocum. "You interested in Hook Fulton?"

"Reckon I am."

Macreedy leaned forward, his voice soft. "Lemme tell you about Fulton. A cowboy got off his seat a bit drunk and stumbled into Hook. Hook fell on his tail, looked foolish goin' down. The cowboy couldn't help laugh. Hook shot him right in the gut. Took twenty minutes to croak." Macreedy stroked his chin. "Now why would I want to talk about Hook Fulton? Why would anyone who liked to stay healthy?" Macreedy, still smiling, went off to serve another customer.

Slocum lifted his glass. Well, he had to try.

Someone took the stool next to him. "The name is Lila." Her voice was low and husky.

She wore a low-cut dress to show her cleavage, and her brown eyes looked wise beyond her years.

"Mind if I join you?" She didn't smile, just reached to the bar, took a glass, and held it out for him to

pour. She had a lot of confidence. She was right,
because she was one sexy filly. Not pretty so much
as sexy. Plenty of flesh on her hips and breasts, but
her waist was slender.

"Thirsty?" he grinned.

"Always thirsty."

A cynical glint lurked in the depths of her brown
eyes. He didn't care for the idea of a saloon lady's
sad story, but guessed her to be about twenty-three,
and that her story might be woeful. He didn't want
to think about it, because he wanted a woman badly.
Damnedest thing—his one glimpse of Janie's body
had put the lust into him.

Janie was off limits, however. A beautiful young
filly, but his mission was not to tumble her, but to
help her. He had thought at the beginning he'd been
helping a cowboy avenge the killing of his family, but
the cowboy became a cowgirl. And the last thing she'd
want at a time like this would be a horny stallion
hanging around. Still, his flesh felt primed for a tussle,
and Lila fit his idea of the body he wanted.

"Where you headed, cowboy?"

"That depends."

"Depends on what?" She held her glass out for
another drink.

"On where Hook Fulton is going."

The glass stopped in mid-air. "You don't look like
a friend of Fulton's."

"That's right."

"Then you got a lotta guts. He's the orneriest, slip-
periest polecat who ever crawled the territory."

Slocum smiled. "Sounds like a good friend of
yours."

"Wouldn't let him within a yard of me. But I seen

him do things. What's the name, cowboy?"

"Slocum. John Slocum."

She drank slowly, her eyes fixed on him. "John Slocum who fought at Little Round Top for Pickett?"

He stared at her.

She gazed off, as if thinking of something far away. "Names stick in my mind, like burrs to wool. A cowboy came through here once, spent a week, stayed drunk mosta the time. When he could get it up, he'd reach for me, and when he couldn't he'd talk. He talked about the War, about the killing of the blue-coats. Told me of one man, a hawkeye with a rifle, who stood near him and did nothing but pick off Union men with stripes. He'd watch this soldier shoot, a dead eye, never wasted a bullet. 'Slocum,' he said, 'the cahoot's name was John Slocum, and he was a Georgia man.'"

Slocum had been looking at her, but seeing something else in his mind. She brought it all back—the cracking of rifles, the groans and cries of dying men, the smoke and noise of the battlefield. He remembered his orders: "Shoot the bastards with stripes." That was his job—mowing them down. And the smell and blood and groans had been part of his dreams for a long time after.

"Who was that cowboy?"

"A Georgia man. Never gave his name. I called him Curly."

Curly. Not enough. He wouldn't be able to dig him up in his mind. There had been a lot of Georgia boys. Now it was all a dim memory except when he dreamed; then it was sharp. For a moment, he thought of the plantation, of his brother and father, both gone; then of the land, and of the carpetbagger judge who got himself judged by Slocum's gun justice.

It was all gone, but somehow you never lost it. It was part of you forever. Even at this moment, with a woman called Lila in a saloon in Whistling Rock, it had all come back.

But you could forget with whiskey and a woman.

"Where's your room?" he asked.

She smiled. "Follow me, Slocum."

He followed her up the stairs, fascinated by the movement of her buttocks. Downstairs, the batwing doors swung open and Janie came in. She saw him with the woman and her face went blank. Then she took a seat at the bar.

Not much of a room, but the bed was big. A pitcher of water, a basin, a whiskey bottle and glasses— nothing personal.

She turned to kiss him, and then stood back, smiling. "I like men like you, Slocum."

"Why?"

"There are the Hook Fultons. And then there are men like you."

He bent down to pull off his boots. "What's that mean?"

Her smile became strange. "There are the killers. And there are men who try to kill the killers. Men like that do wonderful things to my body." She pulled off her clothing. Heavy white breasts with plump nipples, rounded hips, softly rounded belly. And the lovely mound, the light curly brown hair, and the silky pink lips.

He pulled down his buckskins and his flesh was bristling, eager for action. "Looks like your body does wonderful things to mine," he drawled.

"Mighty glad to hear that, Slocum." Her voice was a bit fuzzy from drinking, and her eyes seemed unfocused. She stumbled into him. The impact of her body was searing, and his hands went around her waist and her well-packed buttocks. She was all woman. He pressed against her, and the heat of his erect flesh made her breath come fast. He caressed her breasts, so creamy smooth, then bent to a swollen nipple, touched it with his tongue, again and again. She stood, dreamy. His finger probed between her legs, slipped into the juicy warmth. She sighed with pleasure. Her hand had taken hold of him, and the feel was petal soft. She caressed him, then slipped to her knees, and he felt her lips, kissing, moving up and down, the warmth of her mouth encircling him, caressing him, her tongue dancing. He shut his eyes and yielded to the pleasure, and the harsh memories of the past were wiped out by the sharply mounting excitement of his body. He lifted her, her face dreamy with its own excitement, and brought her to the bed. She fell back on it and he looked at her full, curvy woman's body, the legs spread, the peeping pink lips. He leaned over her, guided his swollen flesh, sliding into the velvet depths. She whimpered at his fullness, flung her arms around his body, while his hands grasped her firm buttocks.

He began his rhythm, and she brought up her hips each time, as if she couldn't bear to part with him. His sharpening tension, after a time, made him start powerful thrusts, and she groaned. But she never stopped her rhythm, and he felt a marvelous pull on him. They went on and on, each stroke bringing him delicious pleasure. Every so often she'd grab him suddenly, as her body tightened as if in agony, and then, finally, he could control the tension no longer, and his body coiled and exploded. She flung herself against him, as if trying to force herself into his body.

When he reached the door, she still lay naked on the bed, which looked wrecked. Her face became serious. "Take care of yourself. Keep a sharp eye out. Fulton will come at you like a fox."

He shut the door gently.

6

Janie was gone.

He didn't like that. He came slowly down the steps and caught Macreedy's eye. "What happened to the kid on the stool?"

Macreedy shrugged. "Ordered a whiskey, never drank it, stomped out after five minutes' mumbling. Mad at something."

Slocum went out into the town baking under the fierce sun. No sign of Janie. He started up the dusty street. She was in a fret. Why? Because he wasted time with saloon ladies? What the hell. Better to tangle with a saloon lady and keep his flesh cooled off. Otherwise, he'd start thinking about her and not the danger of the trail, or of Fulton. Did she consider that? Maybe she didn't like the time he took to get sex out of his system. Too bad about her. His flesh felt peaceful, his mind clear of disturbing memories. It wouldn't be smart for her to snipe at him.

As he passed the general store, he glanced in. Not there. He looked in the restaurant, stroked his chin, then walked to the livery. She was sitting on a bale of hay, a straw in her mouth, watching Hollis drink water from a tin cup. They both turned. Janie stood.

"We're ready to go." Her voice was not friendly

as she pulled the black from its stall.

Hollis grinned. "The young fella is in a hurry. Been chomping all this time."

"In a hurry for a showdown," Slocum said, taking the reins of his roan. "Never pays to be in a hurry for that."

Hollis nodded sagely and, as Slocum swung over the saddle, he glanced back, thinking the smith was a man most likely to die in bed of natural causes.

They trotted to the end of town, took the trail southwest, riding silently, and before long Slocum picked up Fulton's tracks.

Janie paid no attention to him, her eyes roving over the land. To the west lay arroyos, cedars and piñons, and in the distance the big, hump-backed mountains were silhouetted against a buttermilk sky. They stopped to let the horses drink and to fill their canteens at a spring.

"Too bad we couldn't taste some of Mrs. Smith's beef stew," he said regretfully.

"We might have, if you didn't waste time messing around with saloon sluts."

He grimaced. "The lady was no slut. And I ain't wasting time."

"She works in a saloon. She ain't no lily of the valley. And you burn plenty of daylight, drinking and whoring."

He took his hat off, scratched his head. "Them's shocking words, coming from a nice, well-brought-up Texas girl."

"Well-brought-up?" A grim line showed at her pretty mouth. "Just shot the heart out of a skunk named Scarbone. Is that well-brought-up?"

"Yeah, you're a hot pistol, but you're still a young lady, and you oughta keep that in mind."

She stared. "I figger I don't have to be anything till I square things with Fulton."

"Oh, you're a young lady, all right, and best you not forget it."

She shot him a hard look. "Maybe *you're* the one who forgets it."

"What's that mean?" he asked.

"Means whatever you think it. And the thing I can't abide is how you burn up time with those saloon girls. Every time you get into a steamy bed with them, you let Fulton and his men get farther away. Maybe too far to ever catch."

He shook his head. "Now don't fret, Janie. Hook will never get away. We'll track him till he drops or we do. So put your mind at ease."

She took off her hat, and her yellow hair shone. "Don't know why you need those sluts."

He stroked his chin, jarred by her directness. "You're sorta young, Janie, and you don't know how men feel."

"Tell me."

"You're funning, aren't you?"

"There are all sorts of men," she said, "but I'd be interested in knowing what pushes a man like you."

He gazed at her lovely face, and the image of her body flashed into his mind. "What pushes men, Janie, is nature, and the sight of a beautiful woman."

She looked thoughtful. "Do you think of me as a woman, Slocum?"

He grinned. "Hard to think of you as a woman, dressed the way you are, and handling that gun like greased lightning. But I reckon, after seeing you one time as a woman, it's hard not to remember you *are* a woman."

She blushed, and he couldn't help think that if anything revealed her as feminine, it would be blushing.

Then he noticed the smoke, southeast—smoke of a burning wagon.

"What is it?" she asked, startled. "Apaches?"

"Could be. A wagon, a house. Across our trail."

Her face set hard. "Let's do what we have to do."

Again he felt a shot of admiration for her. She was one gutsy girl. He rode carefully, keeping his right protected with brush, rock, trees, alert always for ambush.

The smell of the smoke told Slocum a wagon was burning, and as the smoke thickened, he figured more than one. It meant Apaches and it meant trouble. Was it too late to help the settlers? And if too late, should they take on themselves the danger of rampaging Apaches? No clear decision could be made till they sighted the wagons, and then it might be too late. Too late for the settlers, too late to avoid the redskins. Unless they were pleased by what was found in the wagons, the Apaches would gladly ambush two more of the hated palefaces.

By the time the wagons came into view, the smoke had thinned. No Apaches in sight, but five bodies sprawled near the wagon. Two men with arrows in their bodies, a dead boy, and two women with gunshot wounds in their heads.

Slocum studied the ground. The Apaches had come from behind the thick bush, caught the wagons in the open. A butchery. The settlers had had no warning, and after the men had died, one woman shot the other, then herself. The young boy had been strangled.

The Apaches, cheated of the women, set fire to the wagons, grabbed what they could—whiskey, money; the pockets were turned out—and they went off to drink and carouse.

Slocum, rifle in hand, dismounted, and after scanning the horizon again, moved closer. The settlers with their lined, leathery faces probably were farmers who had pulled up stakes for the richer land in the new territory, but found the end of their trail here. They'd been scalped. The women lay in death, unmolested by the Apaches, who respected their act of bravery.

The broken necks of two bottles revealed the Apaches had lucked into whiskey and were guzzling it and mulling over their booty somewhere over the slope to the right.

Something nicked at his mind that he couldn't figure.

Janie spoke up. "Look how these women died." She was staring at them.

"Finished themselves off rather than let the Apaches get them," he said, rubbing his chin. "After the men and the boy were gone, the women figured they had nothing worth living for."

"Dirty shame," Janie said. Her jaw was hard.

They stood there staring at the shambles. Then Slocum said, "Who did the first killing? I once heard a Comanche say that."

"I don't want to hear that," Janie said harshly.

She looked off to the trees. "How many were there?

Looks like three pony prints."

"Only three. Surprise attack did it."

She stared at the women. "They're dead. They killed themselves, but it was the Apaches that did it."

He nodded. She was deeply moved by what had happened to the women. She stared at them, lying crookedly on the ground, fear still printed on their faces.

"What do you think, Slocum, about taking on these Apaches?"

He rubbed his chin, surprised. "Don't think much of it. Hunting Apaches isn't easy. In fact, it's dangerous. We may never get to Hook Fulton. He's what you're after, right?"

She took a long breath. "Let's bury them first."

The sun was starting down by the time they got the settlers buried, and the act of burying them seemed to have left Janie in a cold rage.

"By now those Apaches are drunk as skunks. There'll never be a better time. I'd like to pay them off for this, Slocum."

He grimaced. He, too, had been touched by the way the women died. The men had been shot with arrows and scalped, the boy strangled. The Apaches would go on. They would raid and scalp, and again the victims would be settlers trying to get to California. And, as Janie said, they were drunk, and this was just about the only time they could be hit. Feeling safe, they'd not be too far, in some cover sleeping off the booze. It was their custom to gulp the booze like water and not stop until they dropped.

"The women didn't know how to protect themselves," she said grimly. "It's up to us to do something."

He thought about it. In a way, this was the fortunes of war. The settlers had to know the dangers they were facing. Apaches pushed out of their land could be merciless.

She was watching him. "I thought you had grit."

He smiled. "It isn't that simple. These settlers knew what it might mean, coming here. The Apache is gonna fight. And fight *mean*."

She glared. "You don't fight by killing women and young ones."

"Our troops fought like that, too."

"In revenge for what *they* did."

He shrugged. He knew the Indian, respected him for his courage, warrior skills, determination to fight and die rather than lose his way of life, and the land he was born to.

"The Apaches will hit again," she said. "More innocent people will die."

That was true. They were not finished. It was not a one-shot raid. There would be others, and in a way, the other killings could fall on his shoulders. It was war to the finish between the white man and red man for the land. There was no end to it. Even if he felt inclined to be peaceful, the Apaches would not be. They wouldn't hesitate to ambush the two palefaces, scalp them, steal their guns and horses.

Finally, there was no way to skirt them. They stood across the trail like a dynamite charge waiting to blow up.

She'd been watching him. "I *know* you have grit, Slocum."

"They might be the splinter of a bigger bunch," he said thoughtfully. "Remember the smoke. Out to raid and run. Their prints go up that slope to the rocks.

Don't know how far they've gone but, if you're game, we'll find out."

"I've been game ever since I saw the women." Her voice was harsh.

"They have guns. Won't be easy pickings," he warned.

"Let's just do it."

He glanced at the sun. It was about three hours before dark. The prints went up the slope, cut through heavy brush, and they tracked them. Then Slocum spotted a thickening of mesquite and rocks and, beyond, what looked like a cave.

"We go the rest of the way on foot," he said softly.

As they went forward, they stayed always behind brush or rock. When he heard the sound of a horse, he put his finger to his lips, crept ahead, moving a few feet at a time, listening. He felt the tension in the cords of his neck. Thick brush and boulders made it clear why the Apaches had picked this place to camp. Rocks for protection and the cave for the horses. His ear was cocked, but he couldn't hear a sound, and that above all made him uneasy. The Apaches must have guzzled a lot of firewater, which he was counting heavily on. The only time he'd been able to surprise an Indian had been after a whiskey spree. An Apache was smart enough to drink where he felt safe. This looked like a haven. They were on level ground in tall grass, the cave only thirty feet away, boulder and brush on either side.

Janie, three feet behind him, had her gun out, and her eyes were snapping, her body alert. Suddenly her gun barked. He threw himself down as a bullet from behind a boulder whistled past his ear. He had nothing to shoot at, and glanced back. A painted body lay face down next to a pitted rock—Janie's bullet. Another crack of gunfire and the bullet sliced his shirtsleeve. It came from the boulder to his left, where a fiercely painted red face stared at him, then ducked for shelter, expecting return fire. Slocum flung his body forward, caught a glimpse of the man's head, and fired, his bullet shearing òff an inch from the skull. The man slipped from the boulder, toppled to the ground, squirmed convulsively, then froze.

Slocum stared at him.

Then came silence.

Janie was on her stomach, gun in hand, three feet to the left of him. Slocum held up his hand. His face was rigid.

"There's one more," she said.

"Probably in the cave with the horses." His voice was strained.

"What is it?" She stared at him. "Are you hit?"

His eyes met hers. "They're not Apaches."

She scowled. "What do you mean? Comanches?"

"Not *Indians* at all," he said.

Her cobalt eyes were dark with puzzlement.

"White men," he said. "I've seen this before. White men, if you could call them men. Outlaws masquerading as Indians, painting themselves, raiding the settlers for money, whiskey, horses."

Her face froze. "But the women! Why'd they kill themselves?"

He considered it. "Thought they were Apaches. They looked it—painted red, feathers, arrows, screaming like banshees. They even used smoke. Wait here."

Keeping an eye on the cave where the last outlaw had to be hiding, he crawled to the man shot by Janie.

He was sprawled with his face in the earth. Slocum turned him. A white man, face painted red, a coarse, thick face with washed-out gray eyes. He wore moccasins, buckskins, a red kerchief around his head. He was a phony Apache. Slocum knew they were phony the instant he glimpsed the painted face of the man on the boulder. He should have known before. Something had nicked at him, he remembered. It was the pockets of the settlers turned out. Apaches wouldn't stoop to strip money from a white man. These were outlaws—hyenas who fed on their own kind.

He crawled back to Janie. "White men."

She glanced at the body. "They're lower than a snake's belly. How do we get the last one?"

Slocum stroked his chin. "Of course, he'd like us to leave him there."

Her face looked fierce. "Two women are dead because of them. He's gotta pay."

Slocum smiled grimly. She was all guts. "We'll smoke him out. Throw in burning brush. Panic the horses. Force him out."

He cut and gathered brush, crept to the cave, and set fire to the brush at the side. When it burned brightly, he signalled Janie. She fired at the mouth of the cave to keep it clear, and he flung the fiery brush in as deeply as he could. After he fired and threw the third brush, the horses inside began their frantic neighing. He could hear them stomping, and he and Janie, pistols in hand, waited behind the rocks, watching the smoke build up.

Two wild-eyed horses, neighing with fear, came galloping out, and then he came, huddled low on a bay gelding, firing wildly.

Janie's hand moved fast. Her bullet hit his head,

and he went suddenly limp. His body danced like a crazy doll on the saddle. Then he slid down and the hooves thudded past his body.

7

Hook Fulton sat in the saloon at Hell's Corner, thinking. The saloon had twelve patrons, three saloon ladies, and the Fulton bunch. Hook was a big man with a broad-boned face scarred by fistfights, and his blunt nose seemed improved by its broken bridge. He had deep-set, dark brown, penetrating eyes, big shoulders, and a hard, lean, narrow-waisted body. He was drinking his fifth shot of whiskey and sat with his back against the wall, a position he favored. He knew the virtues of shooting a man in the back: you didn't face his gun. And if you didn't face a man's gun, you didn't face death. Hook knew a lot about death; he'd been dealing it as long as he could remember. He'd always been fast with a gun, but he was too smart to make the mistake of thinking he was faster than anybody. So Hook played the percentages. He collected fast gunmen: Ironfist Gault, Mule Murphy, Johnny Slate, Hank Bacon, and any strays he could use. Some of his men lounged at the table, keeping an eye on him. That was how he trained them: he was the honcho, he did the scheming, and that was how they knocked off banks and mine payrolls between Kansas and Texas. Sometimes the job netted plenty, and that was why good men came around him.

Though he'd gulped five shots, it didn't show, and he scanned the saloon. Part of Hook always stayed alert; he'd discovered long ago that a man survived by staying just three seconds ahead of the other man.

Now he expected a jasper called Slocum to walk through the doors. That miserable polecat knew how to stick with a trail, and it was worrisome. Him and that two-bit sharpshooting whelp with him. Hook had dimly recognized Slocum, remembered him from a poker game in Abilene: a big, lean blade of a man, with green eyes that never blinked. Looked like a powder keg, and Hook, who had lots of experience sizing up men, made a point of not tangling with Slocum in that game. Even invited him to join the bunch. Now Slocum had teamed up with the O'Neill kid on a vendetta trail. In a way, Fulton thought, things were going right. He wanted the O'Neill kid trailing him, all the way to Santa Fe. Then he thought of O'Malley in Santa Fe, and he chewed his lip. That was one man who made him nervous, him and his eight deadeye gunmen. He lifted his drink and turned to immediate problems. He'd left two men on Lookout Crag to bushwhack Slocum, and both men got staked out by the Apaches. Not much could shake Hook, but when the gruesome image came to his mind of Gleason and Baker frying in the sun, the vultures picking at their eyes, he felt a knife-like stab in his gut. Quickly, he sipped whiskey. Slocum had to be stopped; he'd been on his trail long enough. Almost out of Plainsville, where he'd knocked off O'Neill and the boy. The boy—hell, he didn't want to hit the boy, but he grabbed for the rifle and a bullet from a boy could kill you just as dead as one from a man. The same went for that golden-headed girl who shot Wild Bill.

A gutsy missy, and she'd be alive today, Hook thought, if she hadn't turned the gun on him. A beautiful filly like her—what a waste, shooting her.

He'd just as soon stop and knock off that trailing devil, but couldn't afford much time.

He was carrying a hell of a lot of money, the O'Neill money, and he had to move fast. For a moment, O'Neill flashed in his mind, just before the first bullet hit him. Hook grunted. O'Neill died rotten, but what did it matter? Everyone dies. O'Neill was unlucky. To hell with it. In his time Hook had put a lot of men in the ground, and never thought much about it.

The doors swung open and Hook watched Mule Murphy in his dirty buckskins and scuffed boots clump over to the table and drop into a chair. He lifted the bottle, took a long pull.

Fulton glared at him. "Don't do that again, Mule." His voice was cold.

Mule was surprised. "Do what?"

"Put your sweaty mouth over my whiskey bottle."

Mule was jarred; he was a big, thick-necked bruiser with a square face and bright blue eyes. Anger flashed in those eyes; then, knowing his man, he softened. "Sorry, Hook. It's just that ridin' six hours without a stop leaves a man mighty thirsty." He got up, picked a glass off the bar, and came back to the table.

Hook watched him expectantly.

"They're still comin'," Mule said, as he poured whiskey into the shot glass. "I saw wagons burning and figured the Apaches would grab 'em. But they broke through. Saw them with the glasses."

Hook smiled, and to Mule his mouth looked like a knife scar.

"They ain't easy to stop, those two," Hook said.

"Who the hell *is* this Slocum?" asked Ironfist, who'd been drinking quietly.

Hook looked at him and grinned. He liked having Ironfist around. It gave the Fulton bunch a fearsome rep. When you looked at Ironfist, two things hit you like a rock in the head. One was the size of his fists, great hammer fists that looked like they'd been soaked in brine. And the eyes, the dead blue eyes of a murderer that glittered in his big, almost gorilla-like face.

"I heard about Slocum," said Johnny Slate, a dark-eyed, sinewy man, small for the bunch, but a really fast draw. "A Georgia man. A sharpshooter, an eagle eye with the rifle. They say he was with Quantrill."

Hook nodded. "A dangerous man. I once invited him into the gang. Now he's huntin' us. And that kid with him, the O'Neill kid, did you see that sharpshootin'?"

Ironfist stroked his bristly chin with his thick fingers. "I'll take 'em out, if you want, Hook."

Hook stared. "You don't suppose I want two hot pistols on my ass all the way to Santa Fe?"

Ironfist rose to his feet.

Hook glared at him. "Where you goin'?"

"Gonna take 'em out," Ironfist drawled.

"Sit down," Hook said gruffly. "You may be as big as a barn, but they'd cut you in two before you even thought of your gun. We hafta figure out something."

Ironfist scowled, then slowly sat down. He didn't like to take orders, but Hook was the one man who could get away with it.

"What I can't figger is why Slocum got into this O'Neill business," said Mule. "O'Neill wasn't his kin."

Hook looked at him sorrowfully. "You don't understand much, do you, Mule? Maybe Slocum didn't like the way we treated the O'Neill girl. The blonde. We shot her, remember?"

Mule shook his head. "Hard to forget. Such a sweet-lookin' filly. We coulda had a lot o' fun with her."

Hook's piercing eyes were cold as ice. "She put a bullet in Wild Bill and she was pointin' that iron at me. Sweet-lookin' filly, but she hadda go. And don't-'cha think I hated doin' it."

There was a long silence.

The men picked up their shot glasses and drank.

The other patrons in the saloon played cards, drank at the bar, and talked to the women. Every so often the men would look curiously at the Hook bunch, struck by their bulky size.

It made Hook aware of the members of his gang, and he looked at them: Mule, Slate, Ironfist, Hank—all hard hombres who'd been with him in some hot spots. He could count on them when the bullets were zinging. They were men who didn't lose their nerve. They lived on the edge of death, and they didn't flinch when its smell came at them.

Although Hook Fulton didn't care for his fellow man, as much as he could, he cared for these men.

A man like Slocum worried Hook. He had tried to use Gleason and Baker to wipe out Slocum, and that had come to grief. Hook listened to his hunches, and they told him that Slocum had to be stopped or he'd do a lot of damage. That whelp with Slocum was nothing, but as a team they were dangerous. Look how they'd come through two Apache ambushes. That meant plenty.

He thought about Slocum and the O'Neill kid coming into Hell's Corner, probably in about six hours. Be nice to welcome Slocum with a lead party. He himself couldn't stop; besides, it was not his policy to do the gun work. What the hell was the point of gathering gunmen if *he* had to do the job? He looked at Slate, a fast gun. Murphy was not bright, but all guts and fighting spirit. Ironfist was cunning and perfect for close physical work; his fists were killing weapons. Hank was a good back-up man.

Hook took a deep breath. It was good to be surrounded by men like these; it made you feel you couldn't be beat. So why did Slocum make him uneasy? All it took was a single bullet to put Slocum under a pack of dirt. *But he had to keep the O'Neill kid coming.*

He would work out a scheme to put Slocum in a rendezvous with the local undertaker.

Then Hook saw the saloon lady.

She was young, wore a low-cut yellow dress, and, as she sauntered past the table, looked at the men and smiled. She was pink, peaches and cream, and pretty, not yet deep into the life.

Her eyes went flirtatiously over the men, but the look of Ironfist jarred her, and she stared at him like a bird might at a snake. Then she tore her gaze away, but not before her face had registered fear.

Ironfist, who would have taken no notice of her, now took special notice of her.

"Hey, pusscat," he growled.

She stopped, looked at him, her face taut. She'd never seen anyone like him, except in her nightmares, and here he was, alive and glaring at her.

"C'm'ere, pusscat." His dead blue eyes were on her, and his mouth was twisted in a burlesque of a grin.

Hook's jaw clenched. He didn't like women around while he was thinking of business. The men knew it. Ironfist knew it, too, but the woman's shocked fascination had set Ironfist off. Hook's mind worked to quench a small fire before it became a firestorm.

"Why not let it go, Ironfist?" he said.

The giant nodded, but ignored Fulton, his eyes burning at the girl. "C'm'ere, have a drink, pusscat. Sit on my lap." The girl's eyes widened, and it seemed as if her greatest fears about a monster from her nightmares were about to come into her life. She looked about helplessly, then her gaze fastened on a brawny cowboy in a flat black hat banded with metal studs. "Sonny," she said, and the cowboy, standing at the bar, turned. The girl's piteous look snapped him alert.

"What is it, Mady?" His eyes swept the table where Hook and his men were gathered, but they had no meaning to him. Sonny rustled cattle on a nearby ranch, and came in at sundown sometimes to blow off steam. He had a soft spot in his heart for Mady.

He swaggered toward her, straightening his gunbelt. "Someone botherin' you, Mady?" He figured that if he presented himself as her protector, whoever was sassing her would quiet down, and this would build him up with Mady. She did, after all, reach out to him for help.

The Fulton bunch looked at Sonny, amused. To them there was something comic in this cow hustler swaggering up to them. They ate cowboys like him alive, but he didn't know it.

Ironfist ignored Sonny. "Mady," he rumbled, never

taking his eyes off her. "That's a pretty name. Come and sit on my lap. I got a big surprise for you."

Sonny gazed at Ironfist, confused. He'd never seen a face so menacing; he looked more like a gorilla than a man. But Sonny had guts. It didn't matter, he was thinking, if a man was big as a barn or ugly as a gorilla; a bullet in the right place brought him down to size.

Sonny screwed up his courage. "I don't think the lady's interested, mister."

"I'm talking to the lady." Ironfist didn't look at Sonny.

Hook's mouth tightened.

"Well," said Sonny, "she ain't talking to you."

Ironfist slowly turned glaring eyes on the cowboy, and studied him a moment. "Pipsqueak, why don't you run out and rake up some cow dung?"

Sonny was jolted. Then his hand started for his holster.

Hook's icy voice cut through the silence.

"Hold it, cowboy, I got a gun under this table aimed at your gut."

Sonny froze.

The grandfather clock ticked in the terrible silence.

In the street a dog barked twice.

Nobody moved. It seemed a spell had been cast over everyone.

Then Ironfist pulled his pistol and fired.

Sonny hurtled back against the bar, hitting it, his eyes shocked open in surprise. He looked down at the red spreading stain on his chest, then his eyes slowly went dead.

Hook brought his hands up to the table. They were empty. Mule and Slate had come to their feet, guns drawn, facing the patrons of the saloon, who were looking on in frozen silence.

Hook spoke to Mady, who was staring in horror at Sonny sprawled dead against the bar.

"All you had to do, missy, was set on his lap. You wouldn'a lost your hero." He stood up. "Let's go."

Ironfist sat still, his face sullen. "I want the woman."

Hook stared at him coldly. "No time for that. We gotta ride. We got places to go and people to see. And we gotta get rid of Slocum. We'll find you another pretty missy down the trail." He stared at Ironfist, and it took almost a full minute before the big man dropped his eyes and slipped his gun into his holster.

As they went to the batwing doors, Mule and Johnny Slate, with guns out, kept the saloon covered.

8

From the high slope where Slocum sat, Hell's Corner looked like any other six-bit frontier town, with its two-story buildings huddled on flat ground near a narrow, twisting stream.

Hook and his men would stop there for whiskey, smith work, trail supplies, and whatever else a man like Fulton would stop for.

Slocum stroked his chin; though Fulton didn't bypass a town, he traveled fast. Going somewhere in a hurry. Perhaps it explained why he didn't stop to try to wipe out his pursuers. He surely didn't like anyone breathing down his neck, jostling him, disturbing his sleep. Where he was going and why was a mystery that might be solved at the end of the trail, if he and Janie ever reached it. Because Hook, sooner or later, might pull another ambush. It had to be in the cards.

Slocum rode to the bottom of the slope where Janie, on her big black, had been watching him.

"What's the town like?" she asked.

"Like the others—a hellhole with a sinkful of outlaws, and maybe a few good citizens. But you're not going to find too many decent folk in outlaw country."

"Why not bypass it?"

"We need provisions. And we have to make sure

Hook and his men went through. He could throw a curve, ride south or north. A foxy fella. It'd be dumb to forget that. We gotta stay on our toes."

She shrugged. "All I want is to get Hook in front of my gun."

Slocum smiled. "The way Hook survives is to put *his men* in front of the gun. He goes for the back."

Slocum looked at the sun, an orange-red ball sticking on the horizon, as if it hated to give up its last look at this part of the earth. Slocum, who had an eye for such things, studied the peaks of the great mountain ranges sprawled majestically west, a massive show of nature's force. Then his eyes dropped to the bedraggled wooden shacks huddled to form Hell's Corner. He shook his head.

"What is it?" Janie asked.

Whatever it was, he couldn't put it into words— something about the mystery and beauty of nature, compared to what men built.

Instead, he said, "Let's just keep our eyes open. A mangy town like this is a good one for Hook Fulton's devilment."

As the roan trotted closer, Slocum studied the shacks at the edge of town. One was a livery, now a burned-out hulk, and Slocum didn't like the look of it. He had the habit of mind of putting himself in the place of a bushwhacker, and to him a building like that could be strategic for ambush.

He pulled up and Janie did likewise. She looked to him when it came to trail strategy.

"Don't like the look of that shack," he said.

"Looks empty to me."

He grimaced. "Can you see through it?"

She bit her lip. "What are you thinking?"

"Don't know. If I were Hook, I'd put someone there."

She scowled, but said nothing.

"We can't come into town from the east," he said. "If we come in south, we bypass that empty shack."

She gazed at it thoughtfully. "Fulton's in a hurry. Why should he stop here?"

"Don't know that he would. I'm saying he might, and knowing him, he might set up ambush. He's not one to stick his neck out, so it'd be one of his bunch."

"We could separate," she suggested. "You come from the north, me from the south."

Slocum grinned. She not only had guts, she was smart as a whip. The thought had occurred to him, and if she'd been a man he would have suggested it. She was smarter and faster than most men he knew, but she was a woman, and if, by some wild chance, one of the bunch got her gun, she'd be a goner. Her idea was good. Always good strategy in war not to keep your forces in one place. Besides, he could get there *first* and scout. In spite of her lightning draw and everything else, part of his mind worried about her, and it left him a bit nervy, which could be fatal when it came to split-second action.

"Okay, Janie. You come in south. But don't start for at least ten minutes."

She frowned suspiciously. "Why?"

He scratched his head. "It'll take more time for me to get through that stand of timber on the north side of town."

She looked at it, and nodded.

He put the roan into a jog, but as soon as he got beyond her sight, he nudged the horse and it shot forward. He wanted all the time he could get. There might be nothing out there, but he had to act as if it was loaded with dynamite.

Forty yards from town, he swung off the saddle, tied the reins, moved quietly toward the row of log buildings. He singled out the abandoned livery. Between the alleys, he could see an occasional townee on Main Street, a couple of cowpunchers, a woman in calico, an old-timer smoking a clay pipe on his porch. He huddled against the walls of buildings until he reached the last one, the burned-out livery. It had a front and back entrance, a two-story building, the lower story for stalls and smithy work. It looked innocent enough. Moving noiselessly, in a crouch, he stopped below the window. No sound. Everything looked right, but in his experience that meant nothing. He peered over the edge of the windowsill, and his flesh crawled.

Mule Murphy was on his belly near the door, staring east, rifle in hand, under orders by Hook to cover the trail into town. He smoked a cigarillo, but his eyes were fixed on the horizon. It flashed on Slocum that if he and Janie had come in from the east, they'd be dead ducks by now.

Silently he stepped through the window. Mule turned in a flash, found himself staring into a six-shooter.

"Drop the rifle, Mule."

Mule's light blue eyes stared at him but showed no fear. Slocum couldn't help thinking that Hook picked his men well; Mule was gutsy and hard-headed.

"All right, Slocum." Mule dropped the rifle. "You're one cagy fella. Shoulda expected something like this. But it won't do you much good."

"Not doing you much good either." Slocum's voice was grim. "Now pull your gun with your fingers and drop it." He moved forward, and noticed Mule's eyes go up, and in that moment realized there had to be a back-up, which was why Mule was so cool. He flung himself to the side, moving by instinct, just as the gun exploded from upstairs, splintering the wood where he'd been standing.

Slocum, as he rolled, aimed at the fireburst. A grunt told him he'd hit the target. A body fell with a crash. Slocum whipped about to see Mule, gun in hand, at the floor, raising the barrel to shoot. Slocum's gun barked first and Mule jolted, sat down, and his bright blue eyes looked curiously at Slocum. He put his hand to his reddened shoulder. Slocum had not shot for the kill, just to immobilize.

Mule lay against the wall, bleeding; there was wonder in his voice. "Where in hell did you learn to shoot like that?"

Slocum, still wary, picked up Mule's gun and rifle, threw them out the window, then, hugging the wall, moved to the stairs. The man up there might be wounded, and if so, there was no way to know if he could still use his gun. Many a man on the point of death, Slocum knew, had strength enough to pull a trigger and kill.

Cautiously, Slocum climbed the stairs, gun pointed. In the dim light that came through the small dirty window he could see Hank Bacon, sprawled against the wall, his chest leaking blood, his light brown eyes frozen open.

Slocum drew a deep breath. Two of Hook's henchmen had tried a bushwhacking on the edge of town. It was pure nerve, and only the most brazen outlaws would have tried it.

Slocum pulled a leather thong from his buckskin

pocket and tied Mule's wrists. He lit a havana, put it between Mule's lips. "Doesn't look good for you, Mule."

Mule shrugged philosophically. After a career of stealing and killing, Mule had to figure a day of reckoning must come, Slocum thought. When he had teamed up with Hook, he put his life on the line.

Slocum looked at the wound; not serious, the bleeding would soon stop. He took the kerchief from Mule's neck and tied it tightly around the shoulder.

Mule's eyes were sardonic as he watched Slocum; he knew that a tree waited for him, and such details didn't matter.

"Waitin' to put a bullet in me, eh, Mule?"

Mule puffed the cigar. "You outfoxed us. Hook'll get you sooner or later."

"But you won't be here."

Mule smiled slowly. "I had a good run. You can't live forever."

Slocum studied the square face with the clear blue eyes. It was a pity that Mule Murphy had taken the wrong trail. "Tell me, Mule, why did your bunch hit the O'Neills?"

Mule shifted his position; though his hands were tied, he could still handle the cigar. His lips were tight, as if he intended to keep his mouth shut. Suddenly he shrugged, as if it didn't matter any more. Nothing did. "We hit O'Neill because Hook wanted it."

"Why'd he want it?"

Mule's smile was broad. "O'Neill had a big bag of money salted away."

Slocum leaned forward. "How'd Hook know about the money?"

Mule was surprised. "Dunno. Never thought to ask. He just knew. Told us O'Neill had a lotta loot stashed, and it wouldn't hurt us none to look into it. We trusted Hook. He always knew about money."

Slocum rubbed his chin thoughtfully. How in hell *did* he know? The shadows outside the door were longer. The sun was going down. He had to move faster. "What happened, Mule, when you came onto the O'Neills'?"

Mule looked up lazily. "Don't you know?"

"I wasn't there."

Mule became reminiscent. "We caught O'Neill off guard. Asked him polite-like for the money. He had the balls to deny he had any. His kid was there, a yearling. Too bad; we hadn't figured on the kid. Then Hook said there was no way O'Neill was gonna come out whole, but it would go easier for him if he told about the money." Mule shifted uncomfortably. "O'Neill told him to go to hell. Then Hook shot him in the face. A lotta pain. The boy couldn't stand it and went for the rifle. Almost got it, too. Hook shot him. Something in O'Neill died when he saw that. He grabbed for Hook's gun, and that's when Hook finished him. A nasty killin'. But Hook said that's how he wanted O'Neill to go. Dunno why. Didn't even know the man. Then Hook said, 'Where the hell's the girl?'"

Mule puffed the cigar and, with tied hands, took it from his mouth and looked at it. "A good cigar, Slocum." He thought for a moment. "We found the money in the strongbox under the bed. Gold, three bags of gold. Twenty-five thousand dollars. Where in hell did O'Neill get that kind of money?"

"Then what happened?"

"We made fast tracks, but the O'Neill kids came after us. Tailed us, and started shootin'. Knocked off Pete Jimson. We grabbed the blonde beauty . . . well, you saw what happened. That's when you came in."

Mule looked at Slocum. "Is Hank gone?"

Slocum nodded.

Mule's eyes dropped. His voice was soft. "What are you gonna do with me?"

Slocum could see his eyes, a bit clouded by pain now, and maybe by anxiety. "Put you in the hands of the citizens. They'll give you a fair trial," he said.

"Ironfist shot a cowboy at the saloon," Mule's voice was still low.

Slocum's eyes narrowed. "Well, you didn't do it. Maybe you'll just get the pen."

"And maybe I'll just get a stretched neck," Mule said, and smiled. "Nobody lives forever."

"That's right." Slocum pulled Mule to his feet.

Then he thought of Janie, and it hit him hard that she should, by this time, have showed up. He turned abruptly to Mule. "Where's Hook?"

Mule shrugged. "Been gone four hours. Not a man for waitin' around."

Slocum's voice was harsh. "Who else besides you and your friend upstairs were on this job?"

"Johnny Slate."

"And where in hell was he posted?"

"Covered the south trail." Mule's voice was touched with triumph. "I tole you, Hook figgers the angles. He figgered you were cagy, and might not come in from the east trail. So he put Slate on the south." He looked at his reddened shoulder. "But he didn't figger you'd split from the O'Neill girl."

Slocum stared. O'Neill *girl*. How did Hook know that? He brought his face close to Mule's. "How'd Hook know I was traveling with the O'Neill girl?"

Mule looked puzzled.

"Damn, *I* didn't know she was a girl." Slocum swore. "And you never got a close look at her."

"That's the truth, Slocum. Surprised me, too. Hook called her the O'Neill girl brat. I remember Slate saying, ''tweren't a girl, Hook, shootin' like that.' Hook tole us it was. That O'Neill had two grown girls and a boy." Mule shook his head. "So maybe she dressed like a man and cut her hair. Sure fooled us, but not Hook. He figgered why she'd done it. To tail us."

Slocum's jaws were clenched. So Hook knew all the time what waited for him at O'Neill's. Knew he had two daughters, a boy, and the money. How'd he know? Did their paths crisscross sometime in the past? Had they done a job together? But Mule said Hook didn't know O'Neill. And how *did* O'Neill come into all that gold?

Slocum bit his lip. What the hell was he doing here, jabbering at a time like this? Why wasn't he hightailing after Janie?

The shots fired in the livery had pulled some curious townsmen. Slocum decided to put Mule in their hands and run. He suspected that Slate had stopped Janie on the south side of town. How? With a bullet? Hook Fulton shot women, but only if they pointed a gun. He had probably left orders to knock out Slocum, but grab the girl, if possible, and bring her along. Slocum had a dim memory of seeing Slate in Abilene: taut, hard-bodied, fast.

The townsmen were coming up, scowling.

Slocum picked out one in a Stetson, a rugged man with an honest face.

"The name's Slocum, John Slocum. This man is Mule Murphy, one of Hook Fulton's bunch. Wanted in Kansas and Texas for thieving and other crimes. I'd like to put this man in your hands. Will you guarantee he gets a fair trial?"

A man with a narrow face and a small moustache spoke out. "He's one of the gang that shot Sonny Johnson."

"But *he* didn't do it," said Slocum. "I'm hunting Hook Fulton and I gotta make tracks. Again, I ask, will this man get a fair trial?"

"He'll get a rope," said the moustached man. "Sonny was one of our best boys."

"Hold it, Lemuel," said the man in the Stetson. "Name is Amos Ferris. We got a traveling judge in this county. We'll hold Murphy in our jail till he gets here. I guarantee it. We may be called Hell's Corner, but a man gets a fair shake here. We'll take him." Amos pulled his gun.

As Slocum rode off, he glanced at Mule. His face was stony; he'd already written himself off.

9

Slocum put the roan into a gallop until he found the place where he had parted from Janie. He picked up her prints and followed, his jaw clamped hard, the artery in his forehead pumping. The way he figured it, Johnny Slate, hiding behind a rock, could easily have picked her off. She might be on the trail now, dead or wounded. But Hook knew that Janie was a woman, so chances were he'd tell Slate not to shoot.

Slocum cursed himself for underestimating Hook. He was a smart bastard who figured the angles: that Slocum, expecting ambush, would take the south trail coming into town, since there was timber on the north. He didn't happen to figure that Slocum and the girl would split up, however. Anyway, one of them would fall into his trap.

A half-hour of tracking brought him to where Slate had bagged Janie. Here, where the horse prints dug up the earth. He found Slate's prints behind a thick brush near the trail. He had lurked there until she came, and put a gun on her. They rode off, fast, going southwest.

It had happened, Slocum figured, in the last hour. So, Johnny Slate had Janie, and would be bringing

her to Hook. And Hook Fulton had with him that
monster, Ironfist Gault.

Slocum had seen Ironfist once before, in Abilene.

They had an hour's headway.

Slocum put the spurs to the roan.

An hour headway, and it would soon be dark.

If Slate wanted to try for an ambush, he had enough
rocks and trees for that purpose. As Slocum raced
along the trail, he wondered about Slate, what kind
of a man he was, and why he hadn't waited in Hell's
Corner for Mule. There had to be a fall-back plan,
that was why. Hook Fulton had laid it out. In case a
hitch developed, they would meet somewhere else.
Eagle Crossing would be a likely meeting ground.

As for Slate, he was an outlaw. He'd done his share
of stealing and killing; he was in the Hook Bunch,
wasn't he?

And he wasn't going to treat Janie like she was a
plaster saint. Janie with a gun was a holy terror; without one, she was just a vulnerable young woman.

The sun had dipped behind the great cathedrals of
stone to the west, and purple clung to the topmost
peaks. But from the east massive blue clouds of night
tumbled along, as if driven by a hurricane wind. He
had to make up his mind whether to pitch camp or to
keep going. It depended on the moon. He couldn't
track Slate in the dark. He'd ride, as long as he could,
toward Eagle Crossing, and hope that a high wind
would clear the thick bunch of night clouds whirling
out of the east.

Luck was against Slocum, for the moon did not
come out, not even any stars until, finally, he took
the niche between two boulders and pitched camp. In

spite of his concern about Janie, he felt hunger pangs. Earlier he had bypassed the chance to hunt fresh meat, and so he made do with jerky, beans, biscuits, and coffee. He brushed the roan, stroked his haunches, and the horse, who felt his love, showed his own by shoving his velvet nuzzle hard against Slocum's shoulder. Slocum's mouth tightened and he patted the powerful muscles, thinking how the roan had served him, ready any time to run its heart out.

Slocum lay on his bedroll and gazed at the pitch-black vault of the sky. He lit a cigarillo. He didn't feel sleepy; in fact, he had to fight jumpiness. His instinct was to mount up and gallop to help Janie.

Outside of Plainsville, she'd shot one of the bunch. Her sister, Cathy, had killed Wild Bill. By now, Slate had to believe that Mule and Hank also were gone. The Fulton bunch had been mauled. And Slate, if he were vindictive, could take it out of Janie's hide.

He might be a pig like Hook, and put her through rack and ruin. God help her if she ever fell into the hands of that gorilla, Ironfist.

Slocum took a deep breath. Why work himself into a lather when, in plain fact, he could do nothing till the light of day? By that time, whatever evil Johnny Slate intended would be over and done.

That decision clear in mind, he shut his eyes, prepared to sleep easily, but to his surprise he stayed awake. Her image in his head now was clear and vivid; he could see the piercing, cobalt-blue eyes in the oval face, the crop of golden hair, the shapely figure. And the gutsy way she fought to avenge her family. He thought of how she wept to herself, asking no pity, wanting only to pay off in lead and blood the outlaws who had destroyed her folks.

Now she'd fallen into the bloody hands of one of them.

Slocum twisted and turned, looked fretfully at the sky, wondering what devil was tripping him.

And so, restless sleep until the crack of dawn appeared in the east.

He got up feeling jangled and mean, and saddled the roan. When there was light enough, he started to track.

In two hours of hard riding he reached Eagle Crossing, where the land climbed smoothly to a pyramid of rocks.

He studied the ground. They had been here. The ashes lay deep, suggesting that Slate was canny, he'd concealed the fire. Did he learn here that Mule was out? Or that he was now being trailed?

Slocum decided not to lose precious time by camouflaging his moves. He pushed the roan, and where he could, he took shortcuts.

As he rode, he always scanned the sites of possible ambush.

The sun hit the horizon and flames of orange poured over the sky as from a great can of paint, wildly spilled. He passed through plains of green with white, yellow, and purple wildflowers. The sun climbed, and before long he felt its heat. A scorcher of a day ahead, which meant Slate would have to stop and wet down the horses. He, too, would have to stop, but the roan had great stamina, and could get on with less water than most horses.

A stag and a fawn had stopped to cautiously drink at a nearby stream. An alarm shuddered through their bodies, and they scampered toward cover as a mountain lion, crouched and frustrated, came bursting out of the brush, ran a few useless steps, then stopped. The lion raised its head to stare balefully at Slocum and the roan riding through.

Now the land became tricky as the trail went up and down in slopes. He couldn't see what lay behind the rise until he reached it.

The roan's haunches were drenched, and Slocum felt his shirt sticking to his body.

As he neared the top of the slope, his eyes widened in shock.

Janie was walking slowly toward him. His eyes quickly scanned the surrounding land; rocks and trees on either side of the trail, nothing else. Where in hell was her horse? And why was she walking that slowly? Was she hurt? Had Slate put her through hell and turned her loose? But she didn't seem hurt. As he came closer, where he could make out her features, he saw pain and anxiety in her face. What did it mean? She was sending a message: danger.

Then she called, "Look out, Slocum!"

Ambush! He flung himself to the ground, but it was too late, for the bullet zinged into him and threw him sideways. He felt the pain at his side, but it did not spoil his concentration. Janie, too, flung herself to the ground, expecting a bullet.

Slocum's eyes raked the left, fastened on the big boulder. Perhaps the bullet had come from behind it. He fired, testing; his bullet chipped the rocks. No answering fire. Where in hell was Slate?

His position was bad: open ground. A boulder lay twenty feet to his right. He had to reach it or Slate would chop him full of holes. His side felt sticky with blood.

Then, as if Janie saw where he was looking, she

pointed to the thick brush farther to the left of the rock.

That was what he needed. He pretended a move, his head turned away, but he kept his eyes on the brush. Then Slate, figuring he had a shot, came out to aim, and Slocum's gun, in a blur of movement, fired, and Slate stumbled and dropped. He lay squirming on the ground, brought up his gun to fire again, but Slocum's next shot hit the gun, hurtling it out of his hand. Slocum walked toward him, holding his side. Slate's bullet had seared the flesh of his waist; it was painful, but not a serious wound. The shock was greater than the damage.

Slate had been hurt, but he still could do damage if he got hold of a gun. Much as he wanted to , Slocum didn't dare look toward Janie. Slate had her Colt, too, and all he needed was a moment.

"No wrong moves," he said grimly, keeping his gun on the wounded man.

When he reached Slate, who lay partly behind the brush, he could see Janie's gun stuck in the outlaw's gunbelt. He pulled it and looked at Slate closely for the first time. A sinewy, muscled man with high cheeks, pale gray eyes clouded by pain. He'd been hit in a left rib, and wasn't feeling too good. Slocum picked up Slate's gun and flung it deep into the bushes.

"You're a deadeye," Slate said in a soft voice.

Slocum ignored him, turning to look at Janie walking toward them. He studied her for signs that she'd been manhandled. On his second shot he could have killed Slate, but he wanted him alive, for more reasons than one.

Janie's face, as she came closer, was full of concern. "Are you hurt, Slocum?"

He smiled; it was nice to see her lovely face, the warmth, the grace and strength of her. "It's not bad; looks worse than it feels," he told her.

"Let me see," she commanded. She pulled at his shirt, uncovering the flesh, and he could see the blood and the burn of the bullet. A piece of flesh was gone, but he'd had worse than that, much worse, during the War. The image of the hospital flashed in his mind, but he put it away. He pointed with his gun to Slate, lying there grim-faced.

"Has this polecat hurt you? Tell me the truth." His tone was harsh.

Her blue eyes met his squarely. "No. Didn't lay a finger on me. Just threatened me, if I didn't do what he wanted."

Slocum's jaw clenched. "What'd he want?"

She stared at him. "Go easy, Slocum. He never threatened to touch me. Just to shoot me if I didn't walk toward you." She smiled. "He kept a sharp lookout for you. He couldn't get away from you. Especially with my *slow* horse," she said meaningly. "So, he tried to bushwhack you. Make you think he'd turned me loose, so your guard would be down. And he'd pick you off. But you were too smart for Johnny Slate." She turned to the outlaw, and the pain on his face made her bite her lip.

Slocum looked at her curiously. He knew she hated the Fulton bunch, wanted them all dead, yet she seemed unnerved by Johnny Slate's wound.

Slate was watching them, his teeth clenched, obviously in pain.

"You're gonna bleed to death, mister," Slocum said, "unless we get you to a doctor."

Slate shrugged. "I'm finished, Slocum."

Slocum bent to examine his wound. The bullet was under his third rib, a bad place.

"Maybe I could dig out that bullet. Or get you to a doctor."

Slate shifted in pain. "You'd be saving me for a hanging. What's the point?"

When a man was wounded, sometimes he opened up. Slocum decided to give it a try. "The way I heard it, it was Fulton who did all the shooting at O'Neill's. Right, Slate?"

"He did."

"Maybe it'd just be the pen, Slate."

Slate took a deep breath, and it obviously hurt. "I got some whiskey in my saddlebag. 'Preciate it if you'd get it . . ."

Slocum glanced at Janie. She started to where the horses had been picketed.

Slate's face was pale; his blood was pouring out faster than Slocum expected. Might be a goner, after all. Slocum lit up a cigarillo and held it out. "Want this?"

Slate shook his head. "Just the whiskey."

"How'd Hook happen to hit the O'Neill homestead, Slate?"

Slate squirmed a bit, and a thin smile came to his face. "Don't have time for chitchat. I'll be dead in a coupla minutes. Where's the whiskey?"

"Comin'. You could go clean, Slate."

"Gimme the whiskey, maybe I'll remember."

Slocum took off his shirt, folded it, and put it under Slate's head. When Janie brought the whiskey, he poured some into Slate's mouth. The man took a long swallow and seemed to revive a bit. He took another swallow, then looked at Slocum. "What'd you say?"

"How'd Hook happen to hit O'Neill's place?"

Slate's mouth twisted. "Big money there."

"How'd he know that?"

Slate looked confused; he was sinking. His eyes were clouding.

Slocum leaned forward. "How'd Hook know about the money, Slate?"

Slate stared at him. "It . . . was . . . O'Malley . . . tole him . . ."

Slocum scowled. "Who in hell is O'Malley?"

Suddenly Slate realized he was dying. His face distorted in a queer grin. He spoke slowly, painfully. "Glad . . . to . . . go . . . like this. . . . Hated . . . the rope . . ."

And he died, grinning.

10

Slocum stared at Slate as he died, taking a secret with him.

O'Malley?

Who in hell could he be? O'Malley had told Hook about the money. But how did he know? And where would this O'Malley be?

He turned to Janie, who had been looking at the dead Slate, her eyes flat. "Do you know O'Malley?"

She shook her head.

"Where was Slate going? Did he say?" Slocum asked.

"Santa Fe."

"What else did he say?"

Her eyes pulled away from Slate. "Told me that Hook would be waiting for us at the saloon. That Mule, Hank, and he were under orders to gun you down and bring me into Santa Fe."

Slocum's eyes widened. "And Slate never touched you? You wouldn't expect such a man to treat you like you were a lily of the valley."

"Hook told them nobody was to lay a hand on me."

"That right?" Slocum rubbed his chin. "It sure sets off a couple of questions."

"Like what?"

"This whole thing," said Slocum. "Hook doesn't know your pa, but he kills him in cold blood, a nasty killing. Hook knows about your pa's money. A lotta money. Where'd he get it all? And then, you. The last thing the Fulton boys would do is keep their hands off a good-looking woman. But they're told not to touch you. And now this O'Malley. How'd O'Malley know about the money? What do you make of all this?"

She shook her head slowly. "Don't know, Slocum. Can't figure it." Her eyes slid back to Slate. "We can't leave him like this for the coyotes."

Slocum shrugged. "If it had been me lying there, it wouldn't have worried *him*." He walked to the roan, pulled the shovel and some cloths from the saddlebag. His side hurt. When he came back, she bit her lip.

"Slocum, the way you act, you made me forget you've been hit. Give me those cloths." She soaked them in whiskey and put them against the wound. His gunbelt kept the bandage in place. She took the shovel. "I'll dig. You take it easy."

He almost laughed, but it would be smart not to jump around for a time. There was still blood leakage.

He watched her dig; she was surprisingly strong. When she tried to pull Slate's hulking body into the shallow hole, Slocum leaned over and they did it together.

Before they mounted up, she turned to him. "I'm sorry you got hit."

"Not serious." He had a sturdy body that repaired itself fast.

She glanced toward the grave. "Slate didn't seem to be such a bad guy."

Slocum looked thoughtful. "They all seem all right

when they're facing death. You put a killer in jail, he begins to sound decent. But before that he lived by robbing, killing, and raping. They're hyenas, when you come down to it. And Hook Fulton is the worst."

Her voice went fierce. "Let's get him. He's in Santa Fe, going to wait for us at Cork's Saloon. Slate was to bring me there."

Slocum's face hardened. At last they had a definite place to look.

They mounted up and started to ride.

By noon they had to stop. The sun blazed in the cloudless sky like a giant yellow disk, and everything below sweltered. Not a bird flew. The plants stared piteously at the sky, coyotes whimpered and crawled into the shade of deep crevices; not a snake crawled or an insect chattered.

The horses were drenched and Slocum felt his shirt wet clear through.

"We can't go on in this," he said. Janie's face was flushed, but she was game. She kept her lips tight against complaint.

The ears of the roan went up. Slocum grinned. "Smells water."

Ten minutes more of riding brought them to a clear, twisting stream. The horses moved into it and drank thirstily. Slocum poured water over their steaming bodies. Then he filled the canteens.

"Gotta get this crud off my body," he muttered. "I'll go upstream. You can wash here."

He started upstream, pulling his shirt off. She looked at his bronzed, muscled body.

"Don't leave, Slocum."

He turned.

"Last time you left me all sorts of things happened."

The memory came back of the Apache attack at the stream in Texas. He had expected, at the time, to find Jamie dead. But Jamie turned out to be Janie, a woman, lovely, shapely, and naked. He smiled at the recollection.

"Don't want me to leave?" he said. "How do I get this sweat off?"

"Bathe here." Her eyes were sharp on him.

"But you'll be here."

"Yes."

She smiled easily. "It isn't as if you haven't already seen me."

He grinned. "Never saw a prettier sight."

"I don't like bathing alone. Not after what happened the last time. Might not be so lucky this time."

The idea of frolicking with her had a big appeal for Slocum. He grinned and started to peel.

"What are you doin'?" she demanded.

"Goin' to bathe with you, just as you said."

"Didn't say that." Her face was unsmiling, though he could sense she was amused. "I don't want to be *alone* when I bathe. And I don't want you in the water, separated from your gun. That's when we hit trouble. Now, you just hang around, turn your back while I scrub down. Keep a sharp lookout. Not at me. I won't be long. Then you'll have your turn."

She was one ornery critter, Slocum was thinking, but cute as a ladybug. "Well, just hurry up, 'cause I'm stinkin' clear through."

She laughed, peeled her clothes, cool as can be, not waiting for him to turn his head. When her loose-fitting jeans and the loose shirt fell from her body, he was once again startled at the beauty of her body, the fine shoulders, slender waist, the smooth swell of her hips, the shapeliness of her buttocks and legs. As she scampered into the clear water, the sun made a blazing halo of gold around her hair.

Then Slocum turned, pulled a havana, scratched a lucifer on his thumbnail. He was breathing a bit hard and he puffed at the cigar as if that might lower his body heat. He craved a woman, but none was in sight but Janie, and she was forbidden. If only he had turned away before she'd stripped. Now he was bothered by the image of her body printed on his mind.

It made him grind his teeth. She was a beautiful young girl on a mission of revenge for the slaughter of her family. His job was to help her, not to seduce her. But who was doing the seducing? Why hadn't she let him swim upstream, so he didn't have to see or think about her body? She insisted that he stay, and now she'd planted this craving in him that he had to stifle. It was unfair. Men weren't made of steel. How come she didn't know that?

He crushed the cigar under his boot. "Hurry," he growled.

"What?" she sang out sweetly from the stream.

"I said hurry up, damn it. I don't like just standing here stinking."

There was a pause. "I'm sorry that I kept you standing and stinking." Her voice was close behind him and mocking.

He fought the impulse to grab her, shake her, maybe kiss her. It was the damnedest flow of feelings. He could tell that now she'd taken her things to the nearby bushes. "All right. Now you can go upstream and bathe if you want. I'll be near."

He swung around, thinking she was behind the bush, but part of her was still visible, and he could see a breast with its pink nipple, her flat stomach and golden maiden hair. She turned sharply and moved behind the bushes.

He looked to heaven in despair. She was like an evil temptress dangling the forbidden. It put him in a vile temper, and he cursed to himself as he strode upstream where, peeling his clothes, he jumped into the cool stream and thrashed about. The water cooled his temper but did nothing to reduce his craving. He came out of the water, aware of the excitement of his flesh. He sighed and bent to his clothes, then, sensing a presence, he grabbed his gun on the ground.

It was Janie, twenty yards away. She'd been watching him, her gun out. He brought up his pants, slipped them over his proud male flesh.

"Why in hell didn't you let me know you were there?" he raged.

Her face was deeply blushed. "I . . . told you . . . you'd have your turn. I meant I'd guard you, as you did me."

She turned away. "I'm sorry if I caused any . . ." She stopped. "Oh, the hell with it. Let's get riding."

He put his clothes on.

She couldn't help knowing the effect she had on him, and it had to spoil, to some extent, their easy camaraderie.

Slocum expected to be riding into Santa Fe by the following noon. The heat was so bad that he stopped often to pour water from the canteen into his hat for the horses to drink.

In the afternoon a bunch of cottony clouds floated out of the west to cover the sun and reduce its heat. By mid-afternoon, they had covered a good distance, and found themselves on the trail as it moved narrowly between two high, rocky ridges, forcing them to ride close to each other. With his instinct for danger, Slocum considered this a good ambush site, and he felt uneasy. But he figured that by this time Hook and Ironfist would be swilling whiskey at Cork's Saloon in Santa Fe.

Still, he felt itchy as they navigated the narrow decline, and his eyes kept scanning the cliff tops. Suddenly he was galvanized at the gleam of metal. His gun was out, firing, but the boom of a rifle bounced off the rocks, and the big horse under Janie staggered and seemed to melt toward the ground as Janie jumped clear. A cry of anguish came from her lips as she, too, pulled her gun, looking everywhere to shoot, but seeing nothing. Slocum roweled the roan under an underhanging rock, pulling Janie along, keeping his eyes fastened at the cliff. Nothing. Had he hit the rifleman? It was the second time Janie had lost a horse. The animal kicked its legs futilely in an effort to rise, then lay there, something piteous in its black eyes. Slocum watched the rocks, hoping frantically that a head would appear so he could shoot it off. He looked at Janie, her face screwed in anguish. Tears flowed from her eyes. The horse, on its side, was twisting in agony.

"Please . . ." Janie's voice was wrenched with pain. She turned away as he bent to put a bullet in the brain of the gutted animal.

Slocum's teeth were clenched. The fury he felt could be released in only one way: with the gun. He studied the cliff, there was no way for him to climb it or for the gunman to come down. A standoff. There was a small possibility he could hit the sneaky hyena up there; the rifle had fired before he did. Had he aimed at the horse or at Slocum?

Now what? They'd have to huddle here, wait, then double up on the roan. He ached to get to Santa Fe to smoke out this O'Malley, who seemed to be the cause of Janie O'Neill's misfortunes, and to rip Hook Fulton for all the damage he'd done: three dead O'Neills, two gutted horses. Hook, determined to stop Slocum, had posted another outlaw on that cliff to do his dirty work. Slocum swore silently that, come hell or high water, he'd get into Santa Fe and try to wring Fulton's neck.

His sharp eyes had been watching the cliff top, but could see no movement. Keeping his gun ready, he stepped out from the shelter of the overhanging stone. Still nothing. The rifleman was either hit or had gone.

Janie's face was wet with tears; she'd grown enormously fond of the big black. He, too, felt bad. It was like the death of a faithful, loyal friend. A deep rage burned in him to pay off the outlaw who fired the bullet. He moved to Janie to give her comfort and, without looking at him, she pressed her body against his, her head on his chest, finding consolation in human touch.

Slocum was astonished at his rush of feelings; he wanted to comfort her, to caress her, to hold her tight, kiss her. He felt her breasts hard against his chest, and though he understood that she'd put herself against him because of shock and sorrow, still, as a man, he couldn't help feeling physical excitement. She was a beautiful young woman, and his body recognized it.

They stood together for a few minutes, protected from gunfire by the overhanging rock.

"We've got to go on," he said. "We'll double up on the roan. Keep our guns out till we get past this miserable piece of ground."

She wiped her tears, and her face hardened. "Who d'you s'pose did that shootin', Slocum?"

He shrugged. "Whoever it was, it was Hook's orders. They're trying to stop me. And if they can't get a shot at me, they try to kill the horses."

"Think he's still up there?"

"Don't matter. If he sticks his head out, we'll shoot it off. We just got to ride about five hundred yards; then we'll be clear of ambush."

Her mouth was tight. "He's damned quiet now."

Slocum grinned. "Could be I sliced a piece of him. I shot at something shiny."

"Any man who shoots a horse should be boiled in oil," she said violently.

He smiled. She could combine the kitten with the tiger—quite a girl.

"Let's go, then," she said.

He helped her onto the roan and swung up behind her. He pulled his gun out and looked up to the top of the cliffs as he nudged the horse forward.

Then he became aware of her body in front of him, its warmth and softness. It would be a hard journey, he told himself. He'd have to keep fighting off temptation and focus on the dangers of the trail.

It took almost half an hour for them to get out of range of the attack from the cliff tops. After that, Slocum put his gun into its holster.

The powerful roan jogged along, and Slocum fought to keep his flesh from growing excited against the soft, rounded body in front of him.

Though the roan carried a double burden, they made good headway. And by the time the sun dipped to the horizon, painting giant smears of orange on the sky, Slocum felt that this would be their last night on the trail.

Tomorrow, Santa Fe, where he hoped for a show-down with Hook Fulton.

They made camp at a creek near rocks that, if needed, would serve as cover. Earlier in the day he had shot a pheasant, and the roasted meat tasted good. Afterward, they had coffee, which left a nice glow in his gut.

They watched the sun go down, throwing fiery light on the thin, pitted spires of the mountain and on the great slabs of red rock that seemed to stretch west forever.

Slocum smoked, and the night came fast over the land. Suddenly there was a dark blue canopy above their heads, a million bits of starfire, and the silvery moon throwing light on the stark land around them.

Janie's mood was quiet, and Slocum had no way of knowing her thoughts. She was a quicksilver girl, bright as a butterfly one moment and gloomy as a mule the next. She had, he reckoned, plenty to think about. This time tomorrow the showdown with Hook could be over.

Then Slocum thought of O'Malley. His mind couldn't let it alone.

What part did he play in all this?

O'Malley knew about O'Neill's bags of gold. And Janie didn't know O'Malley, so where did he come

from? It was O'Malley who put Hook on the scent.
Could be that Hook might never have hit the O'Neills
if not for O'Malley. That meant O'Malley was indi-
rectly part of this bloodbath.

11

What stuck in Slocum's mind was something Mule had said: "Hook shot him in the face. A lotta pain ... A nasty killin', but Hook said that's how he wanted O'Neill to go." That was what Mule had said. Then he had added, "Surprising, 'cause Hook didn't even know the man."

Hook didn't even know O'Neill.

Why kill him like that if Hook didn't know him, didn't even have a grievance?

The more Slocum thought about it, the more it seemed that the key to the killing of the O'Neills could be found in the mystery of O'Malley.

"What are you thinkin' about, Slocum?" Janie asked. She'd been watching him in the firelight, and was curious.

"Thinking we'll be in Santa Fe tomorrow."

"Yes." Her lips were tight. "And Hook Fulton will be waitin' for his men to bring me in."

He nodded. "I figure, before we nail Hook—if we do—we have to squeeze out what he knows about O'Malley."

"Why?"

"*He* put Hook onto the money. We got to find the connection."

She frowned. "Why would this man O'Malley put Fulton onto my father?"

"That's what we gotta find out, pretty missy."

Her blue eyes, darkly mysterious, gazed at him. "You think me pretty, Slocum?"

"More than that. Beautiful."

She smiled. "You never said that before."

"Thought it a lotta times."

"Even in these loose ol' rags I'm wearin'?"

He grinned. "Beauty shines through." Then he stroked his chin. "Besides, I did see you without those rags."

Her cheeks, it seemed to him, were a touch red. "And I saw you, too, Slocum."

They gazed at each other. A coyote in the distance let loose a mournful howl. The moon, almost full and silvery, was climbing up the night sky.

"Tomorrow's the showdown." Her voice was husky. "Don't know if we'll be alive tomorrow, this time,"

He said nothing.

"Let's make love, Slocum," she said. "There may never be another time."

He took a deep breath. It was true; anything could happen tomorrow. Hook was a devil, and no matter how careful you were . . . Still, she was so young. Was it right? But death could be so sudden. "Are you sure, Janie?"

"Oh, I'm sure."

She was a beautiful young woman, and he had been craving her for a long time. They could both be dead tomorrow. Meanwhile, they had tonight.

He moved to her, put his arms around her. She lifted her face, offered her lips. She had a sweet, flower-like kissing mouth. He kissed her repeatedly, held her body close. He could feel her breasts against his chest. He unbuttoned her shirt; her breasts were full and round, the nipples erect. She was in a passion. He slipped off her shirt; she had nicely rounded shoulders. He loosened her britches and they dropped. She had a slender waist that curved into voluptuous hips. Her thighs were firm, her calves rounded. He kissed her breasts, put his tongue on her nipples, and she began to breathe fast.

He stopped and whispered, "Take your boots off." As she dropped to the ground and wrestled with them, he quickly stripped, and his maleness stood erect, swollen with passion. She looked at it with wonder.

He pulled her to her feet, entirely nude, her skin glistening white in the moonlight. His hands stroked her body, her waist, buttocks, and his mouth again went to her breasts. Then his finger slipped between her thighs, probing to the moist, silky warmth within; she sighed with pleasure. He put her hand over his swollen flesh, and the petal feel of her palm sharpened his excitement.

He carried her to the blanket, brought his body over hers, and contact with her silky flesh was a shock of pleasure. She flung her arms around him, and as her thighs instinctively parted he brought the tip of his throbbing flesh between, slipped in a bit. She was tight, but could accept his muscular bigness. Though she was virginal, riding seemed to have opened her. Slocum slipped in deeper and her smooth, moist flesh enfolded him. Slowly but insistently he went deeper, while she waited until he was entirely within.

He began his movements gently, not wanting to

hurt her. But nature had her ways, and as he moved, she to began to move and to whimper with pleasure.

His hands were over her breasts, hips, buttocks. She pulled his head down to kiss him, as if to tell him how much pleasure she felt.

Then his rhythm quickened, and though he tried with might and main to slow down, the irresistible surge of excitement became too much. Taking firm hold of her buttocks, he began vigorous thrusts, and he hit his peak and exploded.

A cry broke from her lips as for the first time her body went through agonizing waves of pleasure.

She put her arms around his waist, held him fiercely, as if she wanted his flesh to imprint itself on her forever.

He caressed her face, stayed close.

She was dreamy afterward, and as they lay side by side, looking up at the moon overhead, she said, "Why didn't we do it before, Slocum?"

He just smiled.

She put her hands behind her head, which brought up her breasts. "So much time wasted," she said. "We should have been lovin' long ago." Her eyes turned to him with reproach.

He was startled. "But you had killing Hook Fulton on your mind."

"I still got it," she said fiercely. "But there could have been time for this. And you did nothin'."

He shook his head. *How do you figure a woman?* he wondered. All that time wasted. They could have been loving all along the Santa Fe trail.

He touched her breast, felt a new surge of excitement. "Well, we could make up for lost time," he said.

They made love again. This time he taught her a
couple of tricks, which she found mighty pleasing.
And afterward, she lay in blissful content for a long
time.

Then, in the silence, she said, "I hope I haven't
lost my nerve, Slocum, now that I know about this.
Hope I'm not gonna be a coward this time tomorrow.
Don't like the idea of dyin' and leavin' all this lovin'
behind."

He looked at her, leaning on his elbow. "You ain't
gonna die tomorrow, Janie O'Neill, 'cause I'm gonna
be there."

She kissed him. "Tomorrow, maybe, we'll wipe
Hook Fulton off the face of the earth."

The sun came up strong the next day, and it looked
like another scorcher. Slocum had hoped to be in Santa
Fe just after midday, but he would not punish the roan
in the heat, especially carrying a double burden.

He tried often for the shade, made frequent stops
at water holes. The nearer he got to Santa Fe, the
more his mind worked on the puzzle of the O'Neill
massacre.

It made him seem absent-minded to Janie, and more
than once she glanced curiously at him.

They stopped one more time before Santa Fe, and
after they had coffee, Slocum, who'd been chewing
on the problem, looked into the fire.

"Too bad about Slate," he said.

Her cobalt-blue eyes looked surprised. "What do
you mean?"

"He gave us the name of O'Malley, then dropped
dead."

She said nothing.

"Are you *sure* you never heard of O'Malley? Your pa never mentioned him?"

"Never." She raised the cup to her lips. "Why should my pa mention him?"

"I just thought." He bent to her. "Ever bother you that your pa had such a lot of money?"

"No, just took it for granted. It was always there."

"Ever say how he got it?"

"Sold a lot of good land in East Texas."

Slocum smiled. "Musta sold an awful lot for twenty-five thousand in gold."

She frowned. "No reason to doubt my pa."

He shrugged.

"What's on your mind, Slocum?" she asked.

"To get money like that, you'd have to be a big cattleman or else strike it rich in gold."

She shook her head. "My father lived a quiet life. Liked farming, horses. Most of all, he wanted his kids to be the best with shootin' irons. Had us practicing every afternoon. I've told you."

"How about your ma?"

Janie's face went melancholy. "Died when I was in my teens, in childbirth, giving birth to Johnny. Poor Johnny felt guilty. And he died, trying to defend Dad."

Slocum sipped his coffee. Mother dead in child-birth. Johnny dead, her sister, Cathy, dead. The father dead. She was the only O'Neill survivor. Life sure had treated Janie O'Neill rough. She seemed to be thinking this, too, for her eyes went moist as she realized her family was all gone, struck down by some devil who'd come out of the New Mexico Territory.

Her mouth was tight. "So, who is this O'Malley? Do you have some idea?"

"I figure he knew your father long ago, when he got hold of the money."

"When he got hold of the money," she repeated mechanically. "How do *you* figger my father got that money?"

"Dunno. But when he did, O'Malley seems to have known about it."

"But that was years ago. Why'd he wait so long to come after it?"

"That's the mystery," Slocum said. "If he knew, why'd he wait? Unless..." A thought hit him.

"Unless what?"

"Unless he didn't know where your father was. Maybe it was a kind of feud."

She stared into the fire. "You got some imagination, Slocum. Sounds like you've been smoking loco weed. 'Cause you spun all this outa the name of O'Malley."

Slocum lit a cigar and blew smoke into the air. "Remember what Slate said when I asked, 'How'd Hook know about the money?' And Slate said, 'It was O'Malley tole him.'"

There was a long silence.

His face was grim. "Then Fulton, who didn't personally know your father, came to Texas, shot him up bad. For what reason? 'Cause Fulton was a vicious dog? Yes, partly, but also because that was his orders. There's big money here, and Hook was going to do what he was told."

Her face was hard. "I don't know, Slocum. What you're saying seems to make sense. Maybe yes, maybe no. But we're lookin' for two men now. Hook Fulton and Mr. O'Malley, whoever he is."

12

Sean O'Malley came out of the big stone house of the Bar M ranch onto the spacious porch where his foreman, Barry Gannet, waited. O'Malley nodded, signalled the chair to Gannet, then paused to look out at the land that stretched, mile after mile, as far as the eye could see. A rich, green, smooth, beautiful land with trees, streams, corrals of horses and cattle, a hundred thousand head, and all of it his.

He pulled a cigar from the pocket of his green shirt, lit it, and puffed a few times, his deep blue brooding eyes studying the land. He was tall, with a deeply lined, rugged face, a thick, powerful nose, a hard straight mouth, and curly gray hair.

He turned to Gannet, pulled out another cigar, tossed it, and waited for him to light it.

"Well?" O'Malley said.

"Hook Fulton's at Cork's. Been there the last two nights, waitin'."

"For what?"

"For the girl. Slate or Mule will bring her in, Hook says. A matter of time."

O'Malley's eyes gleamed. "What else?"

"Said he took care of O'Neill the way you wanted. Found the gold—said fifteen thousand."

O'Malley's mouth was hard, but there was a strange glow in his eyes.

"Did he give you details?"

"He said he'd bring the girl, and tell you everything then."

"That's it?"

Gannet shook his head. "Said it was a hard operation. Ran into a hot pistol name of Slocum, who took it on himself to help the girl. Hook lost a couple of men."

O'Malley looked alert. "This Slocum. He's not to be hurt. Ride in and tell Hook to bring Slocum out here, too. How'd *he* get into it?"

"Dunno. It's been bloody. Hook says he's goin' to wait for his men, that he'll be here, likely tonight or tomorrow at the latest."

O'Malley lifted the cigar to his lips. "Well, take him at his word. If he doesn't show tomorrow, take eight men and bring him." He nodded, and Gannet, who knew his man, looked carefully at O'Malley, then walked off the porch to his horse.

O'Malley was silent, thinking of Hook Fulton, a bloody outlaw, and the man he'd chosen to do the job. Looked like he'd done most of it. Took care of Johnny—what had he called himself? John O'Neill: changed his name, of course. Got him, and in the way O'Malley wanted. He could hardly wait to hear what had happened in Plainsville.

Hook got the gold, too, fifteen thousand. That meant he spent a lot. Hard to believe, from the style he lived. Fulton was a thief, but that didn't matter. It was more than the money.

He thought of Grace, and again the scalding anger swept over him, unfaded over the years. And mixed

in, everything else that had happened because of
Johnny, a man he trusted all the way. A terrible lesson,
a lesson learned well: that men had greed and lust in
their hearts.

He sat down on the rocker of the big porch, smoked,
and thought of that hellish day when he'd come home—
he lived in a log cabin then—to find Grace gone.

Gone with Johnny, his own half-brother.

He had never dreamed there'd been anything between them.

And Grace had taken the child.

He read it all in the prints, and started to track
them, after he could calm down enough to think
straight. Then came the great cloudburst, as if God
was working with them, and all tracks were washed
away.

So they got clear, vanished off the face of the earth.
And Johnny had grabbed the gold. The gold they had
taken in the one outlaw act of his life, robbing the
bank in El Paso.

O'Malley had done it for her, for Grace, who wanted
the nice things, hated their poverty. One day Johnny
had brought the plan to him, to hit the bank at night,
after it's monthly gold shipment. To pick up the banker
from his home, where he lived alone, and force him
to open the safe. "We do just this one job, Sean."
Johnny had said. "and we're fixed for life. A stake
for you to buy your ranch and stock it, and a stake
for me."

The plan had been foolproof, because Johnny had
scouted everything carefully, been inconspicuous in
town, followed the banker, a man called Harris, to
his home. So, on a night in spring, after the gold
shipment, they did it, and nobody got hurt: the job

took fifteen minutes. They tied Harris in his office, and three miles out of town changed horses, clothes, and were off scot free.

There was twenty-five thousand dollars in gold coins, enough for them both to live high on the hog. And for Grace, O'Malley's beautiful wife.

How was he to know that she would walk out on him with the money, with his own half-brother, and his only child.

He was sick about it for a long time afterward.

He searched for them in Texas, Colorado, even Kansas, searched for more than a year before giving up.

It changed him. He had once been a soft, gentle, caring man, but he turned, became bitter, secretive, untrusting. He worked like a demon, got land, worked it, traded shrewdly, made deals, then a deal with Phelps, the railroad man, to ship cattle north. Sean O'Malley got richer and richer.

He never married again. And the anger in his heart never healed. Grace and Johnny had done the unforgivable. He must have always known that Johnny didn't play by the rules, that he wanted what he wanted in a hurry.

And Grace taking his two-year-old child. That made him unforgiving.

She'd run off with a daughter he might never see again. How could he pay off such evil?

Many a time he had dreamed of what he'd do, but they were only dreams, and the years slipped by.

Then it happened—what he had thought would never happen—the day when he had the amazing luck to ride through Plainsville, a town he never been to, and saw the man who looked like Johnny just walk into the general store. Older, grayer, stouter, but Johnny.

O'Malley almost sank into the ground. He was petrified. His impulse was to pull his gun, then his years of control took over. He had to learn about Grace, that bitch. And Janie.

By this time Sean O'Malley had a huge ranch and was enormously wealthy. He was a rich, old, and lonely man, and he wanted to leave what he'd built to his own flesh and blood.

So he smothered his anger, lurked in the hotel facing Levy's General Store, and watched Johnny come out. Yes, it was him—grayed, lined, but the same face. He watched him put the supplies in the buckboard and ride north.

Taking great care not to be seen, O'Malley followed the wheel tracks, talking to nobody. No point asking questions which might link him with what he intended to do to Johnny. He'd dreamed for years about how to avenge himself on his half-brother.

The trail led to a nice, secluded property, back in the hills. A fine hideaway, where a man could escape his destiny. O'Malley watched the grounds with field glasses in hope of seeing Grace. But he never saw her. He saw a young woman who looked like her, a younger girl, and a boy. And, finally, behind the house, he saw the grave. So Grace was gone.

But she left children—and one was his—to his worst enemy.

The worst.

The man who had ruined his life.

He had to pay him off.

It was then he thought of Hook Fulton.

* * *

The heat bounced hard off the street as they walked the roan into Santa Fe. A couple of cowboys were herding a few cattle through the streets. Slocum and Janie dismounted and walked alongside the roan. There were four saloons in town, and Cork's was the biggest.

Slocum stopped at the livery, telling the smith, a well-fed, muscular man with a black beard, to fix two shoes on the roan. He also bought a fine-looking white horse with black markings on the chest and legs for Janie.

The liveryman, a man named Cutler, looked pleased at the business.

Slocum asked, "Know a man called O'Malley?"

Cutler stared a moment, then smiled. "You must be from a long way off. O'Malley owns a spread eight miles south of Santa Fe. And about a hundred thousand head of cattle. One of the big honchos out here."

"He is? What about Hook Fulton? Seen him around town?"

Cutler nodded. "Comes in to Cork's every night for drinking and card playing. Likes to gamble, likes to win."

"Ironfist with him?" Slocum asked casually.

"The gorilla? Oh, yes. Always alongside Hook."

They watched the smith finish the work on the roan, thanked him, then rode to Cork's Saloon, not far from the edge of town.

The saloon was a big two-story building in the center of town with a big sign— CORK'S. There were about fifteen horses tied to the rail, mostly good stock. No sign of Hook's piebald or of Ironfist's bay gelding.

Not here yet; but it wouldn't hurt to be prepared for anything. No point expecting Hook to advertise his presence with his piebald. The liveryman said that

Fulton came for the evening card games.

Slocum pushed open the swinging doors, gun hand ready, just in case. It was a big saloon with about twenty-five customers and some women. Men at the card tables and bar. From the second floor, a red-haired woman in a low-cut purple dress showing plenty leaned on the railing and watched the customers. She had a pretty face.

No Hook, no Ironfist. It didn't matter; knowing Hook, any one of the cowboys could be a gunman.

Slocum walked to the middle of the bar, ordered a whiskey, and a few minutes later watched Janie come in, her hand not far from her holster. Slocum's eyes drifted over every man for any sign of recognition. The men played cards or talked to each other.

Slocum poured another whiskey from the bottle in front of him. He told Janie to go to the end of the bar. They were to seem unacquainted.

He watched her walk slowly to the bar, her hat pulled low to conceal her youthful, beardless face. In the company of rough, big, black-bearded men, she couldn't help appear different. It worried Slocum, for he understood the urge of a bully to pick on smaller men. He kept alert to head off any such diversion. Fulton was the target, Slocum had emphasized to her before they came into the saloon. But he had to recognize that someone like her in a rowdy saloon where whiskey fired the blood could be a red flag to a bull.

She had ordered a whiskey and the barman smiled broadly when he put it down, but said nothing. Probably wanted to say it should be spiked with milk, Slocum thought. Then he saw the woman in the purple dress with the splendid bosom come down the stairs and saunter over to Janie.

Slocum lifted his drink, and was amused at the encounter. He could easily listen from his position.

"Hello, cowboy," purred the woman. "Wouldn't you like to buy Cherie a drink?"

Janie's face, sullen when she saw Cherie approach, studied the woman, then smiled. "Sure." She used a low, husky voice.

The barman put out another glass. Cherie smiled broadly and sipped her drink daintily.

"Haven't seen you around here," she said. "Just blow into town?"

Janie nodded, her eyes flicking from Cherie to Slocum.

"Where'd you ride in from, pretty boy?" Cherie asked.

Slocum watched Janie's face harden. "Don't call me that." Her voice was sharp.

Cherie looked puzzled. "Meant no offense, cowboy. You're a mighty good-lookin' young fella. That's all I had in mind."

Janie glanced at Slocum, who threw her a warning look. He had cautioned her about getting off the track with the bar people.

"It's all right, Cherie," Janie said casually.

Cherie smiled, pleased that things were right between them. To Slocum, she seemed smitten by Janie.

Cherie sipped a bit more whiskey. "In my opinion, it's lucky to be good-looking in this world."

Janie stroked her chin, wondering how she could benefit from Cherie's obvious interest. "I'm looking for someone, Cherie. Maybe you can help."

"I'd be glad to help you, cowboy. I like your style.

Janie leaned forward, keeping her voice low. "I wanta get in touch with Hook Fulton. Can you help?".

Cherie's face turned blank, then she became thoughtful. She, too, lowered her voice.

"Can't tell you anything here. You know what I mean. Tell you what you want up there."

Slocum heard part of what she had said, but whatever it was, he could see it seemed to fascinate Janie.

"Go ahead," she said, and with a quick glance at Slocum, she followed Cherie up the stairs to a corridor, where he lost sight of them.

Slocum found the idea of two women in a room, one planning the seduction of the other, a bit funny. He smiled as he imagined what might happen if Cherie, interested in a bit of flesh money, put a hand on Janie.

To kill time, he thought it might be a nice idea to be playing cards when Hook came in.

As he moved to the table, a grizzled man threw his cards down with disgust. "I'm through." He glanced at Slocum. "This chair ain't exactly lucky, friend."

"The luck's about to change." Slocum said.

One big man with a grouchy face said, "Cluett's the name. Nobody's lucky here but me."

"Slocum."

As he played, he kept glancing to the upper floor, expecting Janie would appear. When she didn't, he wondered if Janie found Cherie interesting after all. The idea was idiotic, then suddenly he felt uneasy.

He'd play another round, then go up, but he found himself with a couple of aces. You didn't throw away aces. He bet high, to scare off the others, but three men stayed, obviously holding good cards.

The draw left him with aces and eights. Again he bet high to scare them out, but they stayed, and Cluett stayed to the end, so that when the bets were all down, about seventy-five dollars was in the pile.

Cluett, the big, hulky bruiser, most aggressive in the betting, grinned as he laid down a pair of kings and fours. He reached for the pot, sure he was the winner. When he saw Slocum's aces and eights, he said, "Damn, you're one lucky bastard."

Slocum leaned forward. "Don't think I heard you good, mister. What'd you say?"

Cluett scowled. "Sorry, it slipped. Sorta disappointed. No insult intended."

Slocum shrugged and pulled the money together. He was concerned about Janie, and he stood up.

Cluett stared. "Hope you're not planning to leave, mister."

"Want to check on a friend upstairs," Slocum said.

"Friend upstairs? Talking of Cherie? She'll be there. She ain't goin' places. Just hold on tight." Cluett's face was flushed with whiskey.

Slocum was tempted, for the moment, to relax. It was true: nobody would be going anywhere up there. At least, he'd see it if they did. So why did he have this sense of unease? What in hell was going on?

"Think I'll go up. Won't be gone long."

Cluett pushed his chair back. "Mister, you got a good hunk of my money. And you're gonna play. I don't aim to hear any fancy stories."

Slocum's green eyes drilled into Cluett.

Cluett was a big-chested man with powerful biceps. He was not packing a gun, and he didn't seem intimidated at the idea of fisticuffs. Slocum's mind worked fast. He hated the idea of a long drag-down fight with this pigheaded cowboy. There was no way past him: you had to go through him. It meant a fistfight, a long one, unless he could cut it short.

The men nearby had picked up the threatening tone

in Cluett's voice and were interested in a knockdown fight between the two husky cowboys. Their eyes gleamed with anticipated pleasure.

Cluett's fists were clenched, his face whiskey red, his eyes sullen.

Slocum took a deep breath. "I'm going up there, Cluett, and if you're smart, you won't try to stop me."

Cluett brought his bulky body in front of Slocum. "But I aim to stop you, mister."

When Slocum stepped forward, Cluett swung a powerful right that glanced off Slocum's shoulder. Slocum slipped to his left, brought his fist like a piledriver into the man's gut, which bent him forward, then Slocum hit his jaw with his right, then left, putting the force of his back into it. It was like a mule's kick, for Cluett sat down, his eyes blank, his face slack. Then, in slow motion, his body slipped to the floor and he lay there, eyes closed, deep in slumberland.

The men turned to look at Slocum, who shrugged. "Lucky shot," he mumbled, then went up the stairs, followed by everyone's eyes. He turned the corridor, opened one door, which was empty. The second, across, was locked; he hesitated, then tried the third. It opened on Cherie, sitting on the bed, alone. "Looking for a party?" She smiled. His eyes slitted as he gazed around the room. He walked in.

"Where's the cowboy who came up with you?" he asked.

Her eyes flickered. "Cowboy?"

He grabbed her arms, pulled her close. "Do you want me to wring your neck?"

Now Cherie looked frightened. "He's gone."

"Where?"

"Dunno—with him, Ironfist."

He glared at her. *"Ironfist!* How in hell did he get into this?"

She bit her lip and trembled. "He was waiting here. All the time. For the cowboy."

"What the hell are you talking about? Tell me everything, or you're a dead pigeon."

"Ironfist was here, waiting. Told me he expected a young cowboy to come in. Wanted me to get him up here. Gave me some money."

"What happened?" Slocum's voice was harsh.

"He had a gun out and he took the gun away from the cowboy, tied his hands, gagged him, and took him down the back stairs, where he had horses. Don't know anything more than that."

Slocum was furious, and flung her back so that she spun onto the bed.

So that was how it was done. Hook had been expecting them. He just bypassed Slocum, went for the girl, whom he'd wanted all the time. It was always Janie they wanted. Now they were taking her somewhere—and it had to be to O'Malley's. He'd have to get into that ranch somehow.

But he might head off Ironfist, if he raced. He went out of the room on the run and didn't even see the man standing behind the door, whose gun butt came down on his skull.

There was a star explosion in his head; then darkness rushed in.

13

When he came to, Slocum was aware of an ache in his head. A dull throb, something like ten hangovers. He opened his eyes and found himself looking at a gorilla-like face with dead blue eyes. Ironfist, pointing a gun, held in his big heavy hand.

Slocum shook his head in hope of clearing its ache and its vision, but it didn't help.

"Hurting a bit, Slocum?" asked a jeering voice. Hook Fulton, his broad face flushed, a whiskey bottle in his hand, was sitting at the table. Slocum's eyes flicked to the corner of the room. To his astonishment, he saw a pale-faced Janie with her hands tied.

"Been waiting for you to come round, Slocum," Hook said casually. "Though I'm not crazy about it. I'd just as soon you were dead. But looks like a *friend of mine* wants to talk to you *first*." His smile was deadly. "But gimme the smallest excuse and I'll put you to sleep permanently. You given us a lotta trouble, and I don't need an excuse."

He turned slowly to Janie. "As for you, young lady, well, I thought we'd never get our hands on you. But we did. And you're gonna ride southwest with us a ways. We're goin' down the back stairs, nice and quiet. Tell you this one time—I'll shoot quicker'n a

wink if you try anything. You seen me do it, and I'll
do it again. So be nice and quiet till we're outa town.
We understand each other?"

Slocum, whose head ached fiercely, and who needed
all the time he could get to think straight, was more
than willing.

Janie's eyes were stony, and Slocum's heart went
out to her. When they had finally caught up with
Hook, the hyena who'd destroyed her folks, he had
managed with trickery to tie them up like hogs. It was
a mystery why Hook didn't put a bullet in him right
off. Didn't he know that if Slocum or Janie got near
a gun, he'd be suddenly dead?

Janie stared at Fulton, thinking how easily she had
walked into a trap into Cherie's room where Fulton,
big as life, the man she'd been hunting for, was waiting with a grin and a gun, along with Ironfist. She
could have dropped through the floor. He got her gun,
tied her wrists, and her one hope had been Slocum,
but he, too, walked into the trap. Fulton was a devil.

Hook motioned with his gun, and they went down
the back stairs where, behind the saloon, horses were
tied to the building post.

It took only a few minutes to pick up Slocum's
roan and ride out of town. They headed southwest,
riding for a long time through the dusty gray of sage,
over seared hills spotted with green.

As they rode into the cloudy, darkening afternoon,
Slocum's head began to clear, though the ache hung
on. Hook had expected them in Santa Fe and played
cards openly at Cork's, where he set a wily trap, using
the girl, Cherie, as bait.

It wasn't hard for Slocum to figure out what had
happened back in Cork's. Hook and Ironfist were lurk-

ing in the one locked room, waiting for him. By that
time, they already had Janie tied up. When Slocum
walked into Cherie's room, she was ready to tell him
what Hook had told her. Hook moved noiselessly behind the door, and when Slocum came barging out,
he got a pistol-butt headache.

Now Slocum figured they had to be riding to
O'Malley's. Once again, O'Malley was the mystery.
He seemed to be powerful enough to stop Hook from
putting a bullet in Slocum or Janie. Hook had to know
she was dangerous as a cobra once she got a gun. But
none of this seemed to bother Hook, especially as he
had done the wrist-tying. The knots were there to stay.

They rode through plush green country for a time,
alongside the mountain range. When they stopped to
eat, Ironfist brought out jerky and canned peaches,
and made coffee, but ignored Slocum as he passed
out the tin plates and cups.

Janie scowled at Hook; she tried not to look at
Ironfist. "What about Slocum?" she asked.

"What about him?"

"Doesn't he eat?"

Fulton's piercing eyes flicked to Slocum and his
mouth twisted. "He'll be dead by tomorrow. Why
waste food?"

She bit her lip, then glared. "If he doesn't eat, I
don't."

Hook stared at her thoughtfully, then shrugged. He
nodded at a sullen Ironfist, who put food on a tin plate
and pushed it to Slocum.

"Why do you worry about them, Hook? Ain't worth
it," Ironfist said.

"O'Malley wants them," Hook growled.

"Thought he just wanted the girl." Ironfist looked

at her. She tried not to shiver.

Hook bit his lip, vexed. "Seems to suddenly want him, too. Sent Gannet over personally. I don't like it."

"Why do you have to bring 'em in at all, Hook?"

Hook grinned. "I don't *have* to do anything. But look at it this way. O'Malley told me that all the gold we find at O'Neill's, we keep. We found twenty thousand. O'Malley deserves something for that. He also said there'd be another five thousand for the girl."

Ironfist grunted, poured whiskey into his coffee cup. He stared with hostile eyes at Slocum. "Don't like the look of him. We take care of a lot of grief if we put a bullet in him."

"And what do we tell O'Malley?"

"That he made a break and we hadda shoot."

Slocum listened impassively, bringing the food to his mouth with his tied hands.

Hook shook his head. "O'Malley wouldn't like that. He'd want to know why you let him break away. He's one mean critter, this O'Malley."

"So what?" Ironfist's voice became gently mocking. "Tell him you're sorry. You made a big mistake."

Hook laughed gently. "Ironfist, you don't know the man. He's even tougher than me. And he's got eight of the best guns in the territory working for him. Some are former marshals. They'd be on our tail. Never give up. And there'd be a rope at the end of it."

Slocum couldn't help finding this interchange fascinating. So that was why Hook Fulton had let him live. Fulton was nothing but a murdering errand boy for O'Malley. But what in hell did O'Malley want from Janie? Or from him?

Ironfist ground his boot into the earth. "This job

cost us a lot, Hook. The bunch is gone. And these are the guns that did it. It's crazy to give 'em to O'Malley. What's he gonna do with them?"

Hook rubbed the bridge of his broken nose. "Dunno, but he's not gonna let this polecat go. He pays in blood. O'Malley ain't gonna let him off the hook, not after what I tell him."

"But the bunch is gone, Hook."

Hook smiled cruelly. "Reckon we can start another bunch, Ironfist. And we got twenty thousand in gold. You gotta figure their split is gone, too. It's you and me that gets it." He pointed a thumb at Slocum. "If you think about it *smart*, this polecat has done us a great favor."

Ironfist scowled. "You ain't got much of a heart, Hook. I liked those men."

"Reckon they were good boys, but it's easier to get gunmen than it is to get twenty thousand in gold, Ironfist. Keep that in mind. So we deliver these two. We find out what's on his mind about Slocum." He rubbed his chin. "I figure Slocum deserves a bullet one way or the other. Not because of how he cleaned out the bunch, but because we don't want him tracking us down, after."

Janie had been listening with repulsion, fascinated by the evil that seemed to ooze from Hook. At last, she couldn't help herself.

"You got to be the lowest kind of skunk I ever saw," she said. Hook turned slowly to stare at her, then smiled. "Seems I heard that before, miss. Can't understand it. I'm just an ordinary fella tryin' to get along, trying to get a little fun outa life. And everyone's trying to shoot my head off. Hook Fulton, one of the worst outlaws in Texas, they say. And, look

here, I'm doing a great favor for O'Malley, bringing
a girl like you to him."

Ironfist grumbled. "Don't like the way that filly
talks, Hook. I think I ought to take her britches down
and spank her."

Janie glared at him.

Slocum clenched his fists and twisted his hands at
the rope.

Hook grinned. "She's a mighty cute filly, and it
could be a lotta fun to do that. But, Ironfist, we gotta
keep thinkin' the money is more important than the
filly. But she did shoot the hell outa Wild Bill, and
that's not easy to forget. Let's just see what happens
over at O'Malley's."

They rode for another three hours, then dark clouds
piled up, and suddenly the sky was loaded with thun-
derheads.

"We'd best get shelter, damn it," said Hook. They
made a hard run for the cliffside where, after a quick
search, they found a cave. The rain came down in
sheets, the sky flashed and crackled, and thunder rat-
tled in the mountains. By this time they were huddled
in the cave, watching the slashing rain.

"Make a fire," Hook told Ironfist. "We'll have to
wait this out. Reckon we're holed up for a spell." He
glanced at Slocum thoughtfully. "Mebbe you oughta
tie his feet, too, to keep him outa mischief."

Ironfist grumbled. "Too much trouble. He ain't
goin' nowhere. I'd sort of like him to try, Hook." He
held up his oversized hands.

Hook grinned. "Reckon he'd run into a bit of thunder from those fists." He shook himself, and brought
a couple of whiskey bottles from the saddle, while

the fire crackled and burned brightly.

The rain swept east, but the sky stayed bloated
with clouds, and dark came down. The fire kept them
comfortable, but Hook grumbled a bit and consoled
himself with whiskey. Ironfist drank, too, and more
than once his gaze traveled to Janie, sitting hunched
and silent in a corner. Slocum, too, sat far back in
the cave, glad of the rain and that it gave him what
he needed. He had concealed in his boot a slender
throwing knife. Given the right moment, he might
free his hands. He had to be mighty careful. A knife
never worked as fast as a gun, and Hook was a shrewd
polecat who stayed on top of things.

Ironfist kept drinking and looking at Janie. His face
became sullen, and he went quiet.

It worried Slocum, for it could mean he'd forget
money and start thinking women. Not Hook, but a
weak head like Ironfist. The whiskey could fire him
up, and Hook might not be able to hold him down.
Slocum suddenly felt he didn't have much time. In
fact, he might not make daylight.

He crawled to the corner of the cave and curled
up, his back to the others, as if to keep his body warm
and go to sleep.

Hook looked at him, puzzled, but Ironfist didn't
bother. He drank and stayed moody and silent.

Then, to Slocum's surprise, Janie spoke up. "Tell
me, Fulton. Why does this O'Malley want to see me?"

"Don't know, little lady. It's his business." Hook
was feeling sociable, sitting at the fire with the bottle
in his hand.

"And he's the one told you about the gold in my
pa's place?"

"That's right."

"Do you know how O'Malley knew about that?"

"Don't know. Don't even care."

Her voice took on an edge. "Why'd you shoot my pa?"

Fulton studied her. "To tell the truth, I had nothin' against him, but I reckon O'Malley had plenty."

"Why?"

"Dunno. But he sure had a big hate. I can vouch for that." Hook smiled. "Could be your pa done him wrong."

Her chin went up.

Slocum was hunched up, his boots near his hands. As the others talked, his ears strained to hear any movement. Inch by inch, he brought the edge of the knife out of its holster, and with imperceptible moves brought the edge against the ropes, pressing until he felt the pressure on his wrists loosen as the rope split. His spirits zoomed. He kept his hands together, as if they were still tied.

He had been listening with astonishment to Janie talking to Fulton. But she, too, had begun to realize that he was just a hired killer, and that the force behind him was O'Malley. Above all, she must want to face the man who had ordered the death of her pa.

Ironfist, sodden with enough booze to drop two men, but not showing it visibly, said, "Why do you talk to this bitch? She shot our boy Wild Bill, remember?"

Hook nodded. "Ironfist, your mind isn't exactly first class. Mebbe, you can recall that we did some damage to the little lady's family. She's kinda gutsy, if you think about it."

Ironfist looked surprised, as if he thought about it for the first time. Then he said, "Sorta pretty, too. A damned pretty filly, Hook." He turned up his bottle to drink, then wiped his mouth. "Why'n't we pleasure ourselves with her, Hook? Long as we bring her in alive, it don' matter, huh?"

Hook's eyes slitted. "That's one thing O'Malley tole me not to do, Ironfist. 'She's not to be touched, by you or your men, Hook,' O'Malley said. 'I'm holdin' you responsible, Hook.'"

Ironfist's big face grew sullen. "Don't like that, Hook. Don't like it one damned bit."

"But you're gonna live with it," Hook said grimly.

Ironfist glowered. He knew Hook could outdraw him every day of the year. But he was bored by the rain, he craved a woman, and the liquor had loosened his desires.

Hook stared coldly at the big, gorilla-like man sitting at the fire beside him. "What'cha kickin' about? You got a bag of gold to spend. You can buy yourself fifty saloon girls. Just hang on, Ironfist."

The small dead-blue eyes glinted. "Okay, Hook, guess you know best." He smiled, stood up to look at the rain. "Looks like it's clearin'." He walked past Hook, who had relaxed, sure that Ironfist had recognized the wisdom of his words. But the big, primitive man could think only of the pleasure in front: the girl now, the gold later. As he passed Hook, he turned slightly and swung his huge hand at Hook's jaw. There was a loud crack, Hook's eyes turned up in his head, and he went flat out. Ironfist had once knocked a mule off its feet with one blow of his fist.

He looked down at the unconscious Hook, then turned, and an almost sweet smile twisted his face as his dead-blue eyes gazed at Slocum and Janie.

"Not a nice thing to do, was it? Hook's my friend.

But he don't unnerstand what a man needs. And, lady, this man needs you. Now you jest be nice and we'll get along fine. But if you make me mad, you won't get outa here in good shape. Unnerstand?"

Slocum had turned to watch him, still holding his position, crouched and helplessly tied.

Ironfist moved in front of Janie, bottle in hand, looking at her like a wolf at a rabbit.

"Don't you touch me, you lowdown polecat," she said. "I'd rather be dead."

The smile seemed to melt from his face; he scowled, lifted the bottle to his lips, and drank. Then he rubbed his chin thoughtfully and sat down facing her. "Don't know why the ladies don't like me," he whined. "I'm a nice gentle fella. An' I sure like 'em a lot." Then he grinned. "Lemme tell ya, you're gonna like Iron-fist. Mebbe I'm not the best-looking cowboy in the territory, but mebbe I got somethin' else." His grin became diabolic. "An' you're gonna be my woman." He shoved the bottle at her. "Have a drink. Loosen you up."

Her eyes gleamed with venom. "You gotta be the lowest thing that ever crawled."

His face froze, a dead, horrifying look. He lifted his hand to slap her, but stopped. "You're a good-lookin' filly, but you got rotten manners. But I don't mind. 'Cause we're gonna have a lotta fun." He jerked his thumb at Slocum. "We'll let him watch. If he gives trouble, I'll just twist his neck, which I been wantin' to do anyway."

He stood and pulled off his shirt to show a massive, hairy chest. His pale eyes gleamed. He was so sodden with whiskey and so caught up by the lovely girl tied helplessly in front of him that he didn't notice that

Slocum had turned and was facing him with something shiny in his hand. When Ironfist did see him, his hand started for his gun, and he saw the thing with the glow of fire come streaking through the air, felt the sharp sudden pain as it pierced his flesh and drove in deep. His body shuddered under the shock and he tried to pull out the knife, but he seemed overpowered by weakness. Then rage in his brain percolated to his body, and he started toward Slocum to crush this rotten dog, but his legs collapsed. Then, in agony, he reached for his gun to kill. Straining with his last strength, he got the gun from his holster, triggered it twice, the bullets driving into the earth. He toppled like a massive tree and fell back, his eyes open and lifeless.

14

Janie rushed to Slocum and threw her body against his. He held her for a long moment, aware of her warm, curving flesh. Then he gently disengaged, bent to slip Hook's gun from its holster, and put it in his own. "First things first," he said dryly. He pulled his knife from Ironfist, wiped it, and cut the rope at her wrist.

She grabbed the gun from Slocum's holster, and, her face hard, pointed it at the unconscious Hook.

"Wait," Slocum said.

The gun in her hand quivered as she looked at Hook, almost in peaceful slumber.

"You're right," she said, her face reddening. "Not like this. I want this rotten skunk to see his death, to feel it."

He nodded. If ever a man deserved to die, it was Hook. A ruthless killer, he had wiped out three members of her family. His gun did it, though the command came from O'Malley.

But to shoot him now, while he was an unconscious lump of flesh, would rob her of her revenge, so she could feel right about her dead family.

And then there was O'Malley, the man behind it all.

There had to be an accounting with O'Malley.

He reached into his pocket for the slender leather thongs he always carried, pulled Hook's hands together, and tied the knots.

Then he went out to the horses, the saddlebags, and came back with his own gun and Janie's. He looked down at Ironfist with distaste, pulled him out to the left of the cave. He could be buried later.

Janie was sitting cross-legged, watching Hook.

"Pour some coffee into him, Slocum, so I can kill him. We'll bury them at the same time." Her face was hard, her eyes feverish, because at last she saw the end of the trail.

"I been thinking," he said.

"What!" she flared at him, as if she somehow knew he would want to delay what she wanted most in the world.

He too sat down cross-legged, facing her.

"I know you want to fill this hyena with lead."

"He killed my family. What else can I do?"

"He's gotta go, yes. But at the right time. We could use him to get to O'Malley."

"What do you mean?"

"We just can't ride into that ranch and grab O'Malley. He's got a lot of guns protecting him."

She was silent.

"We can use Hook. He's supposed to be taking us to the ranch. We'll keep a secret gun on Hook so he behaves. When we get O'Malley and Hook together, we'll dig out what's behind all the killing."

She looked thoughtful but uneasy. "I don't know. I'd hate to lose Hook."

He took a havana from his shirt pocket and lit it.

"Suppose we go in without Hook Fulton. O'Malley could deny everything, say that Hook's crazy, that he had nothing to do with it. Unless we got Hook there to put the lie in his teeth."

She nodded slowly. "You're right. Damn it, I sure want to get O'Malley in my sights. He's got plenty of explaining to do."

"Plenty," Slocum said.

He looked at Hook, still sleeping peacefully, lifted his head, and poured cold coffee into his mouth. Hook gagged, coughed, then his eyes shot open.

He was looking into Janie's Colt. His face paled, and he glanced around, rubbed his chin while his mind tried to work out what happened.

"Looks like things have changed since I dozed off. Can I ask—Where's Ironfist?"

"Dead," Janie said coldly. "And you'd be dead, except for Slocum here."

Hook turned slowly and smiled at Slocum. "Thanks." He felt his chin again. "Ironfist hit me. Almost broke my jaw. That dumb ox. Now he's dead. Sure changes everything."

"Sure does, Hook," said Slocum. "Like, you ain't got the gold any more. And your life is hanging on a string." He bent and stared at Hook's yellow-brown eyes. "Now listen close. We're gonna take you to O'Malley, just where you wanted to go. Only you're going to be a nice fella and act like you're doing the taking. We'll check on whether you told us a cock-and-bull story about O'Malley."

Hook shrugged. "Hell, I got nothin' to lose. I'm tellin' the truth."

"Well, tomorrow at dawn you can dig a grave for

your good friend Ironfist. Looks like he made a mistake when he hit you."

Hook grinned sadistically. "His last mistake."

Slocum tied Hook's hands and feet. "To make sure you don't leave this cave tonight. Sleep here. First thing in the morning, we'll drop Ironfist in the ground, and head out to O'Malley's."

A gentle south wind had been pushing at the clouds, and it wasn't long before stars began to appear. Slocum laid out his sleeping gear not far from Janie's bedroll, under an overhanging cliff.

He put his hands behind his head and stared at the sky. It had been a rotten day, from the time Hook laid his pistol butt on his skull. His head still ached, and his side didn't feel that good either. In spite of care and caution, Hook had outwitted them with his setup at Cork's Saloon. In the end, however, they had Hook hogtied, and were ready to lasso O'Malley.

Tomorrow would be showdown day.

He listened to the mournful howl of a nearby coyote and the hoot of a night owl.

"Slocum," Janie said.

"Yes."

"I got a bad feelin' in my bones about tomorrow."

"Why?"

"Don't know. Maybe because of what Hook said. That Dad did something wrong to O'Malley. Could that be true?"

Though he was an outlaw and a killer, Hook Fulton would tell the truth, Slocum felt. There were outlaws who thought lying was a worse crime than killing, and Slocum figured Hook was one of them.

"What do you think, Slocum?"

"I don't know, Janie. Let's hope we find out tomorrow. Everything."

After a silence, Janie's voice, very soft. "Slocum."

"Yes?"

"Can I come to you?"

A tingle went through him. He wanted her, but had felt the strain of the day might have been too much, and the last thing she'd want would be loving. The tone of her voice told him otherwise.

She crawled to his side. "I thought we were goners," she said. "That animal. I'd kill myself rather than let him touch me."

Slocum put his arms around her, felt her breasts against him. He looked at her face, bent to kiss her. Her mouth tasted sweet.

"I want you, Slocum," she breathed into his ear.

He put his hand against her breast, kissed her again, slipped his hand into her shirt to feel the velvet softness. He opened her shirt, kissed her nipple already taut with passion. Quickly they stripped. The sight of her body made his blood leap. Her white flesh seemed to glow in the dark, and his eyes pleasured in the swell of her breasts and curve of her hips, the shape of her thighs and legs. Her mouth came to him hungry for love.

It seemed that closeness to danger and death had wiped out all her girlish shyness, and she reached for him. He was rigid with excitement, and she held him in her palm and, as if overpowered with passion, reached down to fondle and kiss it. He himself, after a time, bent to her body and buried his face between her thighs. They gave each other great pleasure until finally he slipped over her, felt her solid velvet body

under him, the thighs spread. He slipped into her,
delighting in the smooth, moist warmth, and she gasped
at the shock and pleasure as she engulfed his bigness.
He paused, enjoying the sensation, and then began to
move, his hands holding her silky buttocks. She
brought her hips up in perfect rhythm to meet his
thrusts. Powerful feelings surged through him. Then
he would pause to caress her breasts and hips, her
buttocks, anything to prolong the marvelous flow of
pleasure. As his tension began to rise, he again grasped
her buttocks and now, in a fever of desire thrust with
fire and fury, felt the soaring surge and the explosion.
Her body seemed to coil, tighten, then she unleashed
a long, shuddering sigh.

They lay together for a long time. Then she said
in a soft voice, "That was the most beautiful thing
that ever happened to me, Slocum."

15

Next morning, with the dawn, Slocum untied the ropes on Hook Fulton and put a gun on him.

They walked to the piebald, where Slocum, ever cautious, ran a hand in the saddlebag, checking it for a gun. It would be typical of Fulton, a tricky devil, to back himself up with an extra gun.

Janie, who had been at the fire, called to him. "Coffee."

Slocum turned to Hook. "Pull your shovel and start digging. It's got to be a big hole for Ironfist." He started toward Janie.

"Somehow, I don't mind digging Ironfist underground," said Hook, as he worked to pull his shovel. He seemed to have trouble unleashing it, and struggled with the saddlebag. Slocum had reached Ironfist, and the delay made him uneasy. He glanced back just in time to see Hook turn with a Colt, taken mysteriously from the saddlebag. Slocum spun left as Hook fired, the bullet whistling past his head. He dropped to the ground, rolled as Hook fired again, then, as Slocum pulled his own gun, Hook swung over the piebald, spurred it fiercely, turning again to fire, forcing Slocum to roll again, reaching the rock for cover.

The bullets bounced around him and by the time Slocum could peer out, Hook had run his horse behind a cover of rocks and out of the firing sight of Slocum's gun.

The whole incident, which took only minutes, left Slocum cursing violently under his breath.

Janie, who had dropped for cover at the gunfire, was staring at him, and her look made him want to sink into the ground. The gleam in her eyes was unmistakable.

He'd been careless and Hook had been smart. He must have had an extra gun planted in a secret inner pocket of that saddlebag. An extra gun was the edge Fulton always worked for. Slocum cursed himself again for underestimating Fulton. No point pushing after him now; it was too dangerous. Fulton could be planning ambush. No, it would have to be once again a matter of slow tracking.

Janie's cobalt-blue eyes were glinting. She bit her lip to try to control her anger, but it was no use. Her voice was bitter.

"I tole you, Slocum, to let me shoot him. I tole you."

He shrugged. "It still was the right decision. We need Fulton alive to tackle O'Malley."

She glared. "It was Fulton who killed my family. And Fulton alive is a dangerous rattlesnake. He almost put you alongside of Ironfist."

"Almost is not good enough." Slocum's voice was grim. "He won't get away, not as long as his horse leaves tracks."

"So we start all over again," she said wearily.

"Won't be the first time I started again." His jaw was hard.

She heaved a long sigh. "Let's go, then."

"I'll just put Ironfist to rest," he said, walking to his horse for the shovel.

He dug a hole, lugged Ironfist to it, and dropped him in. Then he mumbled, "Lord, you may have had a reason for someone like Ironfist, but I gotta admit, I can't figure it." He shoved in the earth.

He swung over the saddle and looked at the land. It was hilly and rocky, with cottonwoods bulking against a blue sky with patchy clouds. The great cliffs shouldered their way west. The yellow sun was coming up strong.

Though Janie stayed quiet as they rode, he could sense her anger. Hook, as she had said, was the killer, the man who had destroyed her family. Her instinct was to get him; he was the target of her fury. She could never find peace until Fulton had paid in blood.

Slocum felt she had every right to fry him, but, for the time being, she had not come down on him too hard. His eyes searched the trees restlessly, looked over the rocks, the crevices, wherever a man like Fulton would hide. His tracks headed northwest. Why, Slocum wondered, did he take this direction? Slocum's respect for Fulton had jumped; he seemed rarely to make mistakes, and everything he did had a purpose. If he went northwest, it had to be for a reason.

Slocum's eyes searched the land constantly, looking for the unexpected, yet his mind couldn't help going back to his bungle. It was just such small mistakes that put a man in his grave. Ironfist, caught up by lust, had been careless and had paid with his life.

As for Hook, over and over, he had proved himself a deadly opponent. He had hired gunmen, ordered ambush twice, used the saloon girl, Cherie, in a clever gambit. Fulton never stopped thinking about how to put a lasso on the man who pursued him. Why, then, did Slocum insist on underestimating Fulton?

Only a little while back, Fulton had been all smiles and innocence as he wrestled with his saddle shovel and came up instead with a gun spitting bullets. Only Slocum's own instinct to sense trouble, duck, and roll, had saved him. His next mistake could be fatal. He must remain clear-headed.

Hook was riding smart, working for the high ground, making Slocum worry about bushwhacking. Whenever Hook's tracks went toward boulders, high clumps of ground, dense brush, anything that could serve as an ambush site, Slocum took care in his approach. It slowed the going, but it was safer.

Hook's tracks, taking the high ground, led them shortly to a view of a valley stretching a long way northeast. By noon, the sky looked like a sheet of hot blue, and the sun blazed. They stopped for a bite to eat in the shade of a big boulder.

Janie seemed preoccupied, and said little. *She's not happy with me*, Slocum thought.

Over the coffee, he finally said, "I messed it up."

"Anyone can make a mistake, Slocum," she said. "But my feelin' was to shoot him when we had him. I shoulda done it. Now he's runnin' free. No tellin' what damage he'll do."

Slocum nodded; it was true. Fulton had an uncanny knack for anticipating trouble and creating it. The words of the saloon girl came back to him.

"Hook Fulton," she had said, "has been robbing, cheating, and killing up and down the territory for years, and nobody's yet put a finger on him. You're biting off more than you can chew."

Well, Hook might be smart, but he could still be nailed.

"Where do you suppose Fulton is headin'?" she asked.

"Dunno. He seems to be working a great semicircle that might take us back to O'Malley's ranch. I'm hopin'. So let's get goin'."

She studied him. "This time, Slocum, if I get him in my sights, I'm shootin'."

"I wouldn't do that. If we get him, there'll be a rope for him at the end. Without him, we'll never learn the truth about O'Malley. So hold on."

She didn't like it, he could see, and it made him wonder what she'd do if they ever nailed Fulton.

The fact remained that Fulton was not only ornery, but the slickest polecat he'd ever hunted.

They began to ride, and the tracks hugged the side of the cliff, and, as he judged, moved in a great semicircle.

Suddenly, he frowned as he saw the tracks of an unshod pony move behind Fulton's trail. An Apache had picked up Fulton; damn, that meant trouble.

Janie scowled when she saw the tracks. "How old is it?"

"Fresh prints, probably within the last two hours."

A worrisome development. A single wandering Apache was unusual; there might be more. And it would be a bad break for them if the Apache picked off Fulton.

"This Apache is hunting Fulton," he said.

"Good."

He smiled grimly. "We can't let it happen."

"Fulton deserves a good scalpin'," she said.

"Not just yet. I told you."

She grimaced, displeased that they found themselves not in the position of hunting Fulton, but of helping him.

They moved quickly but carefully until they came to a thicket of trees and brush, perfect for camouflage and ambush. They picketed the horses. Before Slocum entered the thicket, a movement in the valley caught his eyes. His keen vision picked up a tiny moving speck miles away. At this distance, the speck made him think it likely, it would be a stagecoach, but it would take an hour before he'd know for sure. It baffled him why a coach would ride so indirect a trail toward Santa Fe, and he wondered for the moment what its starting depot could be. Then he faced the problem up front.

Both Fulton and the Apache were lurking in the thicket. To trail that Apache, he'd have to move with absolute silence; to step on a twig, scratch a rock, brush against a branch would be to an Apache a signal loud as the scream of a hawk. With luck he might be able to do it, but Janie would spoil it. He'd let her come a short way; then she would have to stop and wait.

He put his hands to his lips, then started into the thicket, picking his steps with great care, never placing his foot down until he found soft earth. His gun was poised to fire, his senses alive to every sound and sight. Janie followed and seemed to use the same care; to his surprise, she moved as quietly as he did. Hunting experience had taught her to stalk silently. Now confident that she would not betray their position, he concentrated on what lay ahead: the Apache's pony, tied to a branch, nibbling on grass, the moccasin prints as they moved deep into the tangle of brush, trees, and stone. After long, slow, patient tracking, Slocum stopped, held his position like a statue. He dared not look back at Janie, who he sensed was about twenty feet behind him. His pulse beat hard, and he breathed slowly, fearful that it could be heard by acute ears. He strained his ears for sound but heard nothing, strained his eyes but could see nothing. But he sensed strongly a human presence nearby, and he trusted such feelings.

His eyes checked, over and over, the same ground: rocks, brush, trees. His eyes persistently went back to the rock, to one. The curious look of it; a bronzed, solid rock. *Damn!* The rock began a slow, imperceptible move, and turned into the Apache, whose bronzed, blunt face stared ahead at something, his hand slowly moving back, ready to throw a knife, its wicked blade gleaming.

Slocum's gun barked, and the Apache coughed twice, curled, and fell face down to the earth.

Slocum's gaze slipped forward to where the Apache had been looking; he could see nothing but dense brush. Where in hell was Hook?

Janie came up.

It was then he heard Hook's harsh voice from above.

"Drop the guns or you're dead. Both of you."

Slocum cursed, froze, then dropped his gun. Janie, too, waited a moment, then dropped hers.

Hook Fulton swung down from the heavy branch of a twisted tree only fifteen feet away. Just then the Apache's body moved and Fulton's gun exploded twice;

the Apache's body jumped and went still, as blood pumped out of the holes.

Fulton came forward stealthily, his gun held hard on Slocum, whose taut body was ready for any opening. "Move back," Fulton ordered.

They backed off, and Fulton picked up both guns, put them in his belt holster.

Then his lean, high-cheeked face broke into a broad grin.

"Must say, Slocum, you did me a great favor. That Apache was working hard for my scalp, and he might have got it. I was waitin' for him, but I confess, I never did see him." He grinned. "You may have saved my life, but that don't mean I owe you anything." He waved his gun at them. "One wrong move, and you're dead. Just remember that."

He turned to look down the valley and a strange smile came to his lips. "Somethin' pretty interestin' goin' on down there. Now, we start walking to the horses. You got some gold of mine."

After they got to the horses, Fulton, holding his gun on them, walked to where he could see into the valley. For a long time he studied it, then motioned to them.

"Take a look."

The swirling dust had become a stagecoach, and far behind it, riding hard, were ten horsemen, Apaches. At this distance, though it was impossible to hear, Slocum could tell they were whooping up a fury. His mouth tightened. There was no way that coach could escape. There were four men riding shotgun, so the coach most probably carried a payroll in gold. They had come this way to avoid thieves, desperadoes, but had run instead into Apaches. It was bad luck. The driver was whipping the horses to a frenzied gallop, but as yet there was no shooting, and there wouldn't be until the Apaches came into range.

Slocum, for the first time, looked at Janie. Her face was stony. She had to be furious with Slocum. He had stopped the Apache from killing Fulton, and now, again, they were in his power. That polecat could do with them what he wanted, and in her eyes, was capable of every crime imaginable. She hated him with every fibre of her being. And, because of Slocum, she found herself again in the power of this evil man. No wonder, when she looked at Slocum, she went stone-faced.

Slocum's heart went out to her, but it was fate, the way the dice bounced.

His own life hung by a thread now. Fulton must believe that Slocum wanted to put a rope around his neck, and he had to fear Slocum as his deadliest enemy. Sure, Slocum had saved his life, but that had been only for his purpose, still dangerous to Fulton. Slocum watched Fulton reach into the saddlebag on the roan, lift out the gold pouch, put it into his own saddlebag. "Can't get too much of this stuff," he said, grinning.

Then he pulled a cigarillo from his breast pocket and lit it. "Sit down."

Janie sat on a small rock at least ten feet away, making it clear she wanted nothing to do with either of them.

Fulton just smiled, and puffed on the cigarillo, his shrewd brown eyes studying Slocum as if he had to make up his mind about something. Slocum felt a sting of danger, and was sure that Fulton was about to decide whether to kill him or not. The next few minutes, he felt, would be crucial.

Fulton's eyes were hard. "Could I ask you somethin', Slocum?"

"I got nothin' but time."

"Remains to be seen how much time." Hook's voice was harsh. He was a killer; he'd act in a split second the moment he felt danger.

Fulton kept his gun in one hand and smoked with the other. He pointed the cigarillo at Janie.

"This girl's got a grievance; I don't deny that. She wants blood for blood. And if I was real smart, I'd shoot her right now, 'cause she's like a rattlesnake ready to strike. But, for the time being, I aim to keep her toothless.

"But it's you I don't exactly understand, Slocum. What's *your* play in all this? Nobody did *you* any hurt. Nobody spilled the blood of your kin. It's hard for me to understand if you got a grievance about what happened back there. What is your feelin' exactly?"

Slocum looked at the lean, tough face, the piercing brown eyes. It was, he sensed, a dangerous moment. His life could depend on his answer.

"It's true there's no blood of my kin in this fight. Just figgered I'd help out the little lady here. That's all."

Fulton's sharp eyes never left his face, searching for hidden feelings. But Slocum just smiled easily, the picture of a man who, for the sake of a little excitement, put his gun at the service of a pretty lady, a man who did it for adventure, for the fun of it, maybe for the promise of sex.

But, in truth, Slocum did it because of his hatred for men like Fulton who, in his eyes, fouled the territory with their evil ways, who, if they triumphed, would make the West a criminal society, a place unfit for good men and women to live in peacefully, with hope. Slocum's instinct was to stand hard against the forces of evil, which were incarnate in men like Fulton.

Hook Fulton stared at Slocum, aware that a man like this would always be his enemy, and was dangerous to his survival. His instinct now was to put a bullet in him immediately, but he decided against it for the sake of something better.

He needed Slocum's help, and maybe a man like Slocum could be corrupted, like all men, when it came to gold.

"What d'ye think are the chances of that stagecoach, Slocum? Four men against ten Apaches?"

"Depends how good the men are."

Fulton blew smoke into the air. "Reckon in a half-hour from now, those four men are goin' to be minus their scalps and the Apaches are goin' to have that coach." He puffed again at the cigarillo, flipped it, watched it fall.

"We ought to do something about them Apaches," Slocum said.

"I'm thinkin' about it."

"Once they get that wagon, they may come for us," Slocum said slowly. "They might track the Apache we shot."

"A miserable thought," Fulton said cheerfully.

"You got to be the meanest man who ever crawled the earth," said Janie from tight lips.

Fulton smiled. "Might be. Won't argue with you. See, I'm not going to let the Apaches have that coach. Want to know why? Because it's got gold. Payroll gold in it."

"How do you know that?" Slocum asked.

"It's my business to know these things."

Slocum studied him. "Did you know that coach was headed here?"

"No. I knew it was comin', but not from where. Just a piece of luck, that's all, to be here. No reason to toss such luck away, either." He rubbed his chin. "So, how'd you like to split a payroll of gold—you and me. 'Fraid we can't count on her. She's got too much poison in her blood. What do you think?" Fulton's eyes were twin points of ice.

Slocum knew what was in Fulton's mind. He would never trust Slocum, not in a million years. Use him; then, in the end, wipe him out. But just to get a gun in his hands would turn the world around for Slocum. It was hard to believe that Fulton would do that. He had to have a plan.

Far down in the valley, gunfire echoed against the great rocky cliff. They looked down. Now there were six Apaches and only two shotgun riders.

Fulton grinned. "You know, Slocum, Sean O'Malley is one man I don't want to cross. He hired me to do something, and it wouldn't work out right for me not to do it." Hook measured Slocum, his mind working hard. "Let's just say that O'Malley's got eight fast guns, men like you, working for him. Men who hang on a trail and never give up. I'm not a mulebrain. I'm not goin' to cross O'Malley."

Slocum glanced at Janie. Her face was graven stone.

Then he turned back to Fulton and drew his breath sharply, because Fulton had raised his gun and was pointing it at his heart.

"Pow!" Fulton said. "You're dead!" But he didn't pull the trigger.

Slocum didn't lift an eyebrow.

Janie had turned, her face pale, her eyes gleaming with fear. Knowing Fulton to be a cold-blooded killer, she expected him to shoot, and the blood had drained from her face at Hook's fiendish game.

Hook lowered his gun.

"That's the proposition. You can be a rich man or a dead man, Slocum."

"Better rich than dead," Slocum said grimly.

Hook Fulton nodded slowly. "Now you understand."

They walked to the edge of the cliff and peered down on the bouncing, jostling wagon as the driver whipped the horses frantically. The rider alongside had his shotgun aimed at one of the braves riding up fast and, just as he pulled the trigger, which unleashed a blast that tore the chest off the Apache, he was himself struck by rifle fire from a powerful Apache riding to the right of the wagon.

The driver, desperate, held the reins between his knees as he turned his shotgun at the big Apache, but a bullet from the Indian's rifle struck his throat, and his hand went up to it. Then, in slow motion, he rose and somersaulted off the wagon and he was lost between the wheels.

The big Apache then jumped on the back of the lead horse and pulled roughly on the reins, bringing the team to a snorting, trembling halt.

Three Apaches rode up, slid off their ponies, and looked curiously into the wagon. Then one of them pulled out two leather pouches and they stood around and looked into it.

Suddenly the big Apache stopped and let his gaze go upward slowly along the rim of the cliff. Slocum and Fulton, both with sharp instincts for danger, froze, scarcely breathing, as the Apache's gaze swept past them without pause to make a circle. He calmly said something to one of the Apaches, who put the pouches back into the coach. Then they moved behind the coach and squatted in a circle for a powwow.

Hook smiled. "Guess they're talkin' about buying a lot of guns with that gold. We're goin' to be good citizens and stop those bloodthirsty savages from killin' our people."

Slocum reached into his pocket for a havana and lit it. Hook watched him. "These Apaches just robbed that stagecoach. A nasty thing to do. They just made it legitimate for us to take back that money." He grinned broadly. "Not bad, is it, Slocum?"

"No, not bad at all," he said, and puffed the havana. In his mind, it had been plenty bad, bloodthirsty; four white men had just paid for it with their lives.

Hook seemed to read his mind, for a curious smile came to his lips. "There's no nice way to make a fortune, Slocum. It's a dirty business. The Apaches have made it easy for us."

"But the Apaches are not goin' to be easy, Hook. They know we're here."

Hook was startled. "Why do you say that?"

"That chief, the big one, saw us. He looked past here; that's the way they do it. They have eyes like eagles. You can be sure they know about us. They're not talking about the money. They're talking about the best plan to smoke us out later."

Hook shrugged. "You're probably right. But it don't scare me."

"It should. It's their territory, and we no longer have the edge of surprise."

Hook smiled at him. "You've done a lot of Indian huntin', I know. I got faith in you. That's why you're not dead, Slocum. 'Cause you're gonna do some more Indian huntin'."

Slocum flipped the cigar away. What he wanted was a gun, and he had to seem to play Fulton's game.

"There's four Apaches down there. We got a lot of work cut out to handle that," Slocum said.

"*You* got a lot of work, Slocum."

"What d'ye mean? I take it you're gonna help."

Hook grinned. "You don't think I'm stupid enough to give you a gun and work alongside you?"

Slocum stared at him. "What *do* you aim to do?"

"I aim to let you hunt all by yourself. Of course you'll have a gun; otherwise, you couldn't kill the Apaches. So here's what I plan to do." He scratched his cheek, and grinned comically. "Now jest listen. I take the pretty missy with me. I'm gonna put your gun with your horse down the road a piece, and when I come back, tell you where it is.

"Then I'll take the missy with me while you get down there and clean out those Injuns. You make one wrong move, I'll put a bullet in the little lady. You just believe that I'll do it. It won't be the first time."

Slocum stared at him. Fulton had a fiendish mind. How could he handle such a man?

"When you come back with the money, I give you my word we'll divide it. I'm not greedy. I've always shared with my men on a job. And I will with you. But just remember this: the girl is the hostage. To guarantee you play this game according to my rules." He rubbed his chin thoughtfully. "There's no way around those Apaches, whatever we do. Even if we tried to run, they'd come after us. So you take care of it, while I take care of her."

Slocum's jaw hardened. This polecat had thought it all out, and he had the winning cards. If, after he got the gun, he came back for Janie, Fulton wouldn't think twice about shooting her.

"How do I know the girl will be all right with you, Fulton?"

Hook grinned. "You don't know, except that I say so. I've always been more interested in gold than girls. That's all you need to know. Now, missy, you'll please ride with me."

Janie, who had heard it all, looked pale. Slocum stared hard at her, trying to send a message for her to trust him, that somehow he would make it come right for her. But the message didn't seem to go through. Her face stayed cold and hard as she turned to her horse. Fulton swung over his saddle, took the reins of the roan, and the three horses walked down the trail.

While they were gone, Slocum peered over the edge of the cliff at the Apaches. They had collected their dead for burial and built a fire on the north side of the stagecoach. The muscular Apache with the red band on his long hair was clearly the chief. Slocum watched him closely, but he seemed not to look again to the cliff top. Had he been mistaken? No, that Apache had the instincts of an eagle. He'd spotted human movement on the cliff top and, too clever to look directly, he pretended to scan it. But in that scan, he had picked up the palefaces. The Apaches were in no hurry to attack. They felt confident of their power to pick up the trail of the palefaces any time. To bury their dead was first, to celebrate their victory second, to hunt down the detested palefaces third. And to bring back the treasures to the tribe would be last.

Then he heard the horses returning, just two of them. Janie sat silent on her saddle, watching him.

"All right, Slocum," said Fulton. "Go down about three hundred yards. You'll find your horse, and your gun in the saddlebag. Just keep goin' down. I'm not saying any more. I've said it all."

Slocum, traveling quickly down the trail, found the roan picketed under a cottonwood. The horse looked at him, its big black eyes expressive with meaning. Slocum felt a rush of affection and ran his hand over the powerfully muscled flank. He reached into the saddlebag and pulled out his Colt. The feel of it sent a surge of power through his body. To be without a gun was like to be Samson without his hair, he suddenly thought.

Now, should he gamble, go back and try and nail Fulton? No. He was a desperado, capable of woman killing; he'd done it right in front of Slocum's eyes once before.

Slocum had no choice. It would have to be the Apaches. Four of them, and if he were lucky enough to finish them off, there was no guarantee that Fulton would keep his word.

But he'd have the gold, a big bargaining chip. If he were lucky enough to get the gold, he'd bunk it while he bargained for Janie's freedom. Once he had that, he'd figure a way to grab Fulton.

Slocum heaved a long sigh. He had to trap four cunning Apaches in their own territory, and then the wily Hook Fulton.

Could he do it?

16

Slocum had become a hunter.

He backtracked, going down the trail, past the great side of stone, down through a maze of bushes, boulders, and tall grass. The late sun was sinking toward the horizon, and the clouds glowed with pink fire.

Slocum rode straight in the saddle, his piercing green eyes moving always, reading the signs of nature. His jaw set hard in his strong, square face.

Fate played funny games, he was thinking. He had saved Fulton's life by shooting the Apache. And here he was riding out to hunt down four Apaches to make Fulton rich. But he was really doing it to use the money in a trade-off for Janie.

As for the Apaches, there was nothing wrong with going after them. They had just killed four white men. And the payroll gold in that coach, turned into rifles, would help them kill a lot more, mostly innocent settlers.

He had tangled before with Apaches, and knew their fighting ways. In daylight he could not match their cunning, their knowledge of the land. His one chance must be the element of surprise.

That meant a night attack. The Indian tried not to

fight at night, believing that death left his spirit lost
and wandering.

So all Slocum could do was make an approach, try
to stay unseen, and wait for the dark. He counted on
a quarter moon, not too bright.

He rode on the valley floor until he reached a secluded spot with boulder, brush, and good grass. He
picketed the roan, patted his flank, and the beautiful
black eyes looked at him as the horse tossed his head.
Slocum checked his gun and began to go forward,
slowly, carefully.

He didn't expect the Apaches to move until they
finished their burial rites. He had to be in the vicinity
of the coach before dark. Slocum had noted two men
with rifles, the chief, and another muscled brave. The
two without rifles had bows and arrows. His hope was
to find them together in a circle around a fire. If he
shot from the dark, they would have no target. If he
didn't find them together, so much the worse for him.

As he moved silently toward the position of the
stagecoach, the sun went down in a flame, and he lay
quietly in the deep grass watching. Then the dark
purple rushed over the skies, the quarter moon shone
in the east, and big, bright stars popped out of the
great spread of blue.

Now, in the dark, he crept softly, fiercely attentive
to avoid sound, aware how quickly the Apache picked
it up.

When finally he caught the glow of the distant
Apache fire, he moved more slowly. Moving in a
crouch, he would take several steps, freeze, and listen.
He moved with limitless patience, like an Apache
trailing its prey. Guttural words picked up by a stray
breeze floated out, and there was calm in the voices.

He kept moving, merging whenever he could with the silhouette of a brush, a tree trunk, a stone, until the dim outline of the stagecoach came in sight. Now he took longer between each step. He became aware of his own breathing, and sometimes held his breath, for fear it might be heard. The play of light from the fire brightened, and he felt new fear that the firelight might hit the metal of his gun or bounce off his skin, catching an Apache's eye.

The Apaches had made their fire twenty feet north of the stagecoach, and his plan was to approach from the south, shoot from between the wheels. The coach could give cover. By now, working on elbow and stomach through tall grass, he had reached thirty feet south of the coach, and peering under the carriage he could see the fire blazing, also the red-banded head tops of the Apaches. They were eating and talking, and one of them suddenly laughed.

By lifting his head just a bit, he could see the bronzed faces, but not clearly, because the flames danced with light and shade. He wanted first to hit the chief, the one with the rifle, the most dangerous. No point waiting; they might pick him up. It was go now, and the best attack would be the rush, to shock them, hit them close up, so each bullet would count.

He rose to a crouch, and then the horse neighed, bringing one of the Apaches to his feet. It was too late to stop—all or nothing now! Gun cocked, he went under the carriage, between the wheels, gun blazing as the Apaches, in shock, tried to rise, grabbing for rifle or tomahawk, but he was shooting chest high and his bullets flung them back, twisting and squirming, and, as they fell, he fired again. *Three!* The other—where was he? They lay still, the blood pumping out of the bulletholes. Still in a crouch, moving, he flung himself behind a nearby rock, out of the light of the fire, and then the rifle fire came, splintering the rock. A pause, and Slocum shot quickly in the direction of the rifle fire, heard a grunt, then silence. He had a hit, but what kind? A wounded man could still kill. He breathed deeply, aware now that his face was wet with sweat. He glanced at the Apaches: they were sprawled on their sides, the blood still oozing from their wounds. No chief; he'd got away. It was he who, at the sound of the neigh, moved quickest. He was out in the dark with a rifle. He would be trouble. He was quick, strong, cunning. Would he attack, or nurse his wound and hold out till daylight? It was night, and they hated to fight at night. What would he do?

Then Slocum heard the horse, at least a hundred feet away. He could see nothing, just hear the hoofbeats headed north. No, the Apache didn't care to fight at night; he'd withdrawn from the field of battle to lick his wound. But he'd be back; of that Slocum was certain. It was in the code—revenge or death.

Slocum looked into the coach. Two leather pouches, a payroll, tagged to be delivered to the bank at Santa Fe.

He lifted the pouches and started to backtrack. The quarter moon had shifted in the sky, and the light was dim. It was pointless in this dark to try to get back to the high ground, to Janie. He'd wait till dawn, bunk the gold, and try to barter her freedom. And look for the chance to trip up Fulton. He had a gun, and it gave him power.

He lugged the pouches until he reached the roan, and heaved a sigh of relief. He had feared the Apache might have stumbled into the horse, but he had gone north.

He felt bone weary and pulled his bedroll, set it under the shelter of an outcropping rock, and lay there looking at the stars. There was no counting on too much sleep with an Apache prowling. He'd have to sleep with one eye open till dawn. Then Fulton. Up to now, he hadn't been able to nail Fulton. A tricky devil. Fulton seemed to fear just one man—O'Malley. Didn't want to cross him. What was his job for O'Malley? It was still a puzzle. But if he could bring Fulton in, maybe it would all come clear. There had to be a way.

He slept restlessly, one ear cocked for human sound. And, at the crack of dawn, he was relieved to find he was still in one piece.

It was after he picked up the trail to the high ground that the pony tracks appeared. He'd been on the look-out for them since he opened his eyes, and the sight of the tracks sent a shot of fear down his spine. That Apache, in search of the paleface, remembered what he'd seen on the rim of the cliff, and, with the break of dawn, he'd started for them.

Thinking of the revenge an Apache would take on the hated palefaces, especially after the slaughter of his comrades, Slocum felt a stab of dread.

Janie!

He roweled the roan, urging him forward, and the powerful horse went swiftly up the slope with great strides. Always fearful of the Apache's ability to hear, Slocum dismounted a long way from the top of the cliff. In his crouch, he moved silently as a ghost toward the top. He heard a man's cry of pain.

It would be Fulton; the Apache had him. What about Janie? Slocum's instinct was to rush, but he was convinced once the Apache heard him he'd finish them both off. He had to keep control, and come silent; he had to have the edge of surprise.

Again he heard the cry of pain. Now he had reached the tall grass, and came forward softly, silently, then raised his head.

The Apache had Fulton tied, bare-backed, to the tree trunk, and, with a fiendish grin, he was showing him the knife. Slocum could see Janie lying unconscious on the ground nearby. He was near enough.

He stood up, stepped forward, and waited.

The Apache, whose rage had concentrated on Fulton, froze at the sound. His rifle was on the ground.

Slocum just waited.

The Apache then made his move, turned and twisted, grabbing his rifle, bringing its barrel up to shoot as Slocum's gun barked once.

A crimson hole bloomed suddenly in the Apache's right eye. He teetered almost like a tightrope walker, slid slowly to the earth, quivered a moment, then lay still, his one good eye staring emptily at heaven.

Walking swiftly forward, Slocum bent to Janie. A bruise was on her forehead where she'd been struck. Her face was pale, but she breathed normally. She'd be all right.

He turned to Fulton. His back was bleeding lightly from two cuts.

"'Bout time you got here, Slocum."

Slocum flashed him a hard look, bent to pick up Fulton's gun.

"Second time you saved my life. I'm thinkin' you can have the gold all for yourself, if you want."

Slocum walked to his saddlebag, pulled a whiskey bottle.

"Untie me, Slocum," Fulton said.

Slocum smiled, "I like the way you look tied, Fulton." He emptied Fulton's gun, put it in his gunbelt, then brought the liquor to Janie's lips.

She opened her eyes and sat up, put her hand to her head. "It hurts."

He leaned forward and kissed it. "Feel any better?" He smiled.

She smiled at him, then looked at Fulton, still tied to the tree. Her eyes grew cold.

"He's still alive," she said.

Slocum lifted her. "And he stays alive till we get to O'Malley. Try to remember, Janie, that O'Malley is the man behind the death of your family. Hook Fulton was just the gun. We got to solve the mystery of O'Malley. As for Fulton, his teeth are pulled."

He dusted himself off. "We're all going to the Bar M."

17

Some time before they got to the Bar M, O'Malley's ranch, Slocum untied Fulton and put a gun, without bullets, in his holster. Slocum's green eyes fixed on Hook with a deadly gleam.

"Act like you're taking us in, Hook. I'll have a gun inside my shirt. One wrong move, and I'll blow your head off."

A high slope gave them a long view of the ranch, and the beauty of it almost took Janie's breath away. Green, rich-looking grass stretching for miles, a big white stone house, corrals of horses, immense herds of grazing cattle, a long, winding stream.

A man of wealth and power, this O'Malley, Slocum thought as he stared at it.

As they rode in, Slocum noted seven men lolling around the fence of a horse corral, big, lean, hard-eyed men in brown vests, buckskins, black hats, all wearing guns. Not cowboys, Slocum thought; more like troubleshooters for O'Malley. It had been smart to use Hook to get past men like these.

One of the men, gray-haired, with lean, high cheeks sauntered toward them, looking sharply at Janie. Then he looked at Slocum, finally at Hook.

Hook grinned, his manner natural. "Tole you, Gannet, I'd bring 'em in."

"'Bout time, Hook. We'll go up to the house. Mr. O'Malley's been waitin'."

Slocum had been watching Hook for the smallest giveaway, but he played his part right.

As they walked to the big house, Gannet turned to Janie. "Have any trouble getting here, miss?" His voice was soft and polite.

Janie was startled at his manner, and for one wild moment she thought of saying she'd gone through hell to get here. But she could feel Slocum's eyes on her, and she just smiled. "No trouble."

"You're Slocum, I suppose. I'm Gannet, foreman of this spread. Mr. O'Malley is interested in meeting you."

And I'm interested as all hell in meeting him, Slocum thought. He just nodded.

They walked into a huge living room with a chandelier, a big wall mirror, oak furniture, and a plush red rug. *O'Malley sure lives good,* Slocum thought.

"Can I offer you some wine?" Gannet said.

Janie turned a cold eye on him. This smooth-talking foreman was too polite. Not the kind of reception she'd been expecting. One idea burned in her mind about O'Malley, and everything else was hogwash.

The door opened and O'Malley stood at the threshold. Slocum had had no way of knowing how he would look; but he was startled by his appearance. A handsome, gray-haired man with dark blue eyes and a strong jaw. He wore a blue denim shirt, jeans, and boots, which to Slocum seemed casual for the man who owned the Bar M. Nothing fake in this hombre.

Though he looked rock-hard, he didn't seem the kind of man who'd send Hook on an errand of killing. But how could you know? There was something faintly familiar about the look of him. His gaze went directly to Janie, and though his expression, that of a cool, controlled man, didn't change, Slocum sensed a strong flow of feelings under it.

Somewhat mystifying, and it sent a few wild ideas ricocheting through Slocum's mind. He stayed alert, aware that Janie did, too. She was not buffaloed by the polite reception. Her family had been killed, and the two men responsible were in this room.

"I'm Sean O'Malley. I'm glad to meet you, Janie."

"My name," she said harshly, "is Jane O'Neill. No one gave you the right to call me anything else."

His eyebrows went up, but his face stayed solemn. He seemed to be tolerant of her obvious anger. He turned. "Mr. Slocum, I'm glad to make your acquaintance."

"That remains to be seen." Slocum's voice was grim.

Again O'Malley seemed willing to ignore the challenge. His gaze drifted to Hook, and his face lost its geniality. "I think you've done your job. And you have your money. You can go."

Hook stood his ground and grimaced. "But I don't have the money. Slocum has it."

Slocum's hand moved like a snake, and his gun was out. "Just so you know who's in charge here, mister," he said.

O'Malley glanced at Gannet, who smiled. "I don't have a gun, Slocum; neither does Gannet. And I suppose Hook's gun has no bullets?"

"That's right, mister. And *we're* here to ask the questions."

O'Malley walked coolly to a chair and sat down. "You could never get out alive, Slocum. My men surround this house, each of them a dead shot. Look out any window if you don't believe me."

Slocum gritted his teeth. It had to be true. A man like O'Malley wouldn't leave anything to chance. Still, he edged to the window. Two of the tall, lean men were visible just outside the window, and they had their guns out.

"Just remember," Slocum growled. "They're out there, but you're in here."

Then Janie spoke. "Don't give a damn about them. I want you to answer one question, O'Malley. Did you hire Hook Fulton to shoot my father?"

"No," O'Malley said.

Slocum shot a glance at Hook, who had been smiling, and looked suddenly bewildered. It was hard to believe that Fulton was faking.

Janie swung to Hook. "Then you were lying, you rotten hyena!"

"O'Malley!" Hook pleaded, aware that, in the next moment, the girl could shoot him.

"Hold it, Janie." O'Malley spoke evenly. He paused, and looked at her with an extraordinary expression in his eyes. "How could I send him to shoot your father? *When I'm your father.*"

The silence in the room was palpable. No one moved.

Janie just stared at O'Malley as if he had lost his mind.

Slocum, who was rocked to his heels, also stared,

and suddenly he believed. There was an actual family resemblance: in the faces, the eye color, the shape of nose and mouth. It sounded crazy, but there was a real physical tie.

Janie, however, could see nothing of this. All she could think of was John O'Neill, the man she'd always known as her father for as long as she had memory.

"You're loco," she said.

"I don't expect you to remember. You were just two years old when I lost you." O'Malley's voice was mournful. Then he turned to Gannet. "Take Hook out."

"Hold it," Slocum said. "Hook is goin' nowhere. He's done a lotta killin' and he's gonna pay."

O'Malley's face became stern, and now he looked like the boss of the Bar M. "I didn't say Hook was going anywhere. He'll be around." He turned to Gannet. "Keep him handy."

Hook's face blanched. "I did a rotten job for you, O'Malley. I lost my men. I haven't got a dime for all I did. I expect you to keep your word."

O'Malley's face was hard. "I will keep my word, if you followed my instructions." He looked at Gannet, who pulled Hook toward the door.

Janie, bewildered by what was happening, looked for guidance at Slocum. She hated the idea that Hook had just moved beyond the reach of her gun. But O'Malley's statement had so shocked her that she felt paralyzed. Slocum didn't seem disturbed about Fulton; he seemed more interested in what O'Malley would say next.

She thought of what had happened back in Plainsville.

"O'Malley," she said, her voice icy. "Hook Fulton

rode into Plainsville last week and shot my father, my brother, and later on, my sister, Cathy. Did you know that?"

A genuine look of pain appeared on O'Malley's face. His eyes shut for a moment, then opened, and, to Slocum's amazement, his eyes were moist. He turned and walked abruptly to the window.

"Gannet," he said sharply.

His foreman, standing with two of the gunmen, came to the window. O'Malley leaned over and talked to him in a low voice for a full minute. Gannet nodded, his face expressionless.

Then O'Malley came back, poured wine in three glasses, and put them down.

"Please," he said.

They ignored the wine and waited for him as he sipped his drink. "I want to say, Slocum, that I'm grateful to you for protecting Janie. I know you both went through a lot."

Janie just watched him. He had said something so wild, so ridiculous, so unimaginable, that she felt petrified, and could do nothing.

"I'm just going to tell you part of a story," O'Malley said. "Sixteen years ago, you were two years old, lived with me and your mother, Grace O'Malley, in a log cabin in Texas. We had hard times.

"One day, John O'Malley, my half-brother, who later called himself John O'Neill, came to me and talked of a great opportunity to get a lot of gold."

"I was poor, you were a little girl, and your mother wanted the good things in life. To make it short, I went in with him, we picked up twenty-five thousand dollars in gold, and nobody got hurt.

"And two nights later, when I was out rounding

my few cattle, John persuaded your mother to go off with him. You were a girl of two with blazing gold hair and gorgeous blue eyes."

He stood up, walked to a drawer, and pulled out a pair of baby socks. He turned. "Do you still have that scar on your right knee when you fell on a sharp rock?"

Janie, who until then had been listening as if in a trance, suddenly shivered, and her cobalt-blue eyes took on an extraordinary glow.

O'Malley's face looked twisted with pain as he remembered a long-gone time. "Johnny took my wife, my precious little girl whom I loved more than life itself, and the gold. Took it all. Why'd he do it? I'll never know. Maybe he felt a grievance against my father, who favored me and never him.

"And so I lost my wife, my babe, and my fortune. Oh, I went after them with a rifle, but a storm wiped out their tracks. Lost them forever, I thought.

"So I started from scratch. A changed man. A hard man. With hard work and hard thought, I built all this. But I never had a day of happiness. Never married again. Never had another child.

"I never forgot John O'Malley. So that, when one day I had the crazy luck to go through Plainsville and saw him, I knew what had to be done. I had to reclaim what was mine. My child, grown up, was there. I wanted her. And I wanted him punished. Grace was gone, I found out. That's when I thought of Hook Fulton." Suddenly he stopped.

Janie was too shocked to talk. She just stared at this man who had had horrible things done to him, and who, in revenge, had ordered horrible things to be done.

She was profoundly moved, and couldn't yet digest the idea that this man could be her real father.

Although the anger she felt toward him was gone, he was, she believed, still responsible for what had happened to Cathy and little Johnny, and they were innocent.

"Your man, Hook Fulton," she said harshly, "shot my brother and sister."

O'Malley shook his head, his eyes bleak. "I had given him strict orders that he was only to handle John O'Neill. Told him he could keep whatever gold he found. There should be a lot, but if not, I'd make it up to him. Told him not to hurt anyone else."

"You told him," she said bitterly, "but they're dead and he's living."

O'Malley took a long breath, walked to the window, looked out. He turned. "Would you both please come here?"

He lifted the curtain for them. On a big oak tree, fifty yards away, Hook Fulton's body dangled.

"I had warned him. He had to pay."

Janie kept staring. Hook's legs and hands had been tied, and his neck was twisted to the side. The killer she had been hunting was now dead.

The lump of gall that, since the day of the shootings, had stuck in her chest, suddenly seemed dissolved.

O'Malley watched her. "I'm an old, rich, lonely man. I've been robbed of my daughter. She's here now. And everything I have is hers, if she wants it." His eyes pleaded. "Will you stay, Janie?"

She stared out the window, but saw nothing.

Both men watched her, and to O'Malley the silence was unbearable.

She turned finally to look at him. Her father, her real flesh-and-blood father, the man responsible for her existence. A quiver of feeling swept over her, as if a long-forgotten, buried memory of someone who loved her had just become alive again. But there were other feelings, too.

"I don't know," she finally said. "It's too quick. Right now I'm numb. I can't forget that you were still part of what happened to my sister and my brother. I need time to think. Time for the hurt to heal."

O'Malley's face was grim. "As long as you haven't said no, Janie." He paused, then asked softly, "Will you at least stay the night?"

She saw in his face the love of her real father. And she nodded.

His face brightened. He turned to Slocum.

"I can't thank you enough for protecting my daughter. I know you both went through hell. Is there anything I can do? Anything?"

Slocum smiled. "You can make Janie happy, if she decides to stay."

O'Malley's strong, hard face broke out into an unexpectedly radiant smile. He put out his hands to Slocum.

Now Slocum took a deep breath. He had come to an end. "Well," he said, and walked through the door, out of the house, toward his horse.

The tall, lean men seemed to know things were all right. They were gathered in a knot at the corral, watching him.

Janie came after him. "Where the hell are you going, Slocum?" she demanded.

"I'm a traveling man," he said. "You've always known it."

A flurry of pain came over her face. "But you're the best thing that ever happened to me." Her eyes had misted.

He looked into her face and had a flash of memory of all the tough, terrible, and beautiful times they had gone through together.

"My sweet little Janie," he said, almost sadly. "You're one of the nicest things that ever happened to me." He cleared his throat, raised his chin. "You still got growing up to do. And someday I'll be traveling through here."

"Slocum," she said, "how can you leave me? After all we've gone through together. How can I face tomorrow without you?"

He kissed her lightly on the cheek and smiled. "Tomorrow is another day," he said.

He swung over his horse, a powerful, lean, bronze-faced man, and started to ride.

She watched him until he was a small speck against the great majestic mountains that looked eternal as they towered against a bright blue sky.

JAKE LOGAN

___	0-867-21087	**SLOCUM'S REVENGE**	$1.95
___	07296-3	**THE JACKSON HOLE TROUBLE**	$2.50
___	07182-0	**SLOCUM AND THE CATTLE QUEEN**	$2.75
___	06413-1	**SLOCUM GETS EVEN**	$2.50
___	06744-0	**SLOCUM AND THE LOST DUTCHMAN MINE**	$2.50
___	07018-2	**BANDIT GOLD**	$2.50
___	06846-3	**GUNS OF THE SOUTH PASS**	$2.50
___	07046-8	**SLOCUM AND THE HATCHET MEN**	$2.50
___	07258-4	**DALLAS MADAM**	$2.50
___	07139-1	**SOUTH OF THE BORDER**	$2.50
___	07460-9	**SLOCUM'S CRIME**	$2.50
___	07567-2	**SLOCUM'S PRIDE**	$2.50
___	07382-3	**SLOCUM AND THE GUN-RUNNERS**	$2.50
___	07494-3	**SLOCUM'S WINNING HAND**	$2.50
___	08382-9	**SLOCUM IN DEADWOOD**	$2.50
___	07753-5	**THE JOURNEY OF DEATH**	$2.50
___	07683-0	**GUNPLAY AT HOBB'S HOLE**	$2.50
___	07654-7	**SLOCUM'S STAMPEDE**	$2.50
___	07784-5	**SLOCUM'S GOOD DEED**	$2.50
___	08101-X	**THE NEVADA SWINDLE**	$2.50

Prices may be slightly higher in Canada.

Available at your local bookstore or return this form to:

 BERKLEY
Book Mailing Service
P.O. Box 690, Rockville Centre, NY 11571

Please send me the titles checked above. I enclose _____ Include 75¢ for postage and handling if one book is ordered; 25¢ per book for two or more not to exceed $1.75. California, Illinois, New York and Tennessee residents please add sales tax.

NAME_____

ADDRESS_____

CITY_____ STATE/ZIP_____

(allow six weeks for delivery)   **162b**